Soaring High

A Julie Classic
Volume 2

by Megan McDonald

★ American Girl®

Questions or comments? Call 1-800-845-0005, visit **americangirl.com**,
or write to Customer Service, American Girl,
8400 Fairway Place, Middleton, WI 53562.

Printed in China
14 15 16 17 18 19 20 LEO 10 9 8 7 6 5 4 3 2 1

All American Girl marks, Beforever™, Julie®, Julie Albright™,
Ivy™, and Ivy Ling™ are trademarks of American Girl.

Cover image by Michael Dwornik and Juliana Kolesova

Cataloging-in-Publication Data available from the Library of Congress

In Memory of John and Mary Louise McDonald

Beforever

Beforever is about making connections.
It's about exploring the past, finding your
place in the present, and thinking about the
possibilities your future can bring. And it's about
seeing the common thread that ties girls from
all times together. The inspiring characters you
will meet stand up for what they care about
most: Helping others. Protecting the earth.
Overcoming injustice. Through their courageous
stories, discover how staying true to your own
beliefs will help make your world better
today—and tomorrow.

TABLE *of* CONTENTS

A Cry in the Park

✿ CHAPTER 1 ✿

 ulie Albright picked up the phone and called her best friend. "Ivy, you have to come over right away. I'm sick!"

"What do you have?" Ivy asked.

"Spring fever!" Julie practically shouted.

While Julie waited for her friend to be dropped off, she scrubbed her sister Tracy's old bike and her own. The blue and chrome gleamed in the early April sunshine. Julie pumped air into the tires as Ivy hopped out of her mom's car.

Ivy pointed to streaks of grease under Julie's eyes. "You look like a raccoon," she teased.

"Make that grease monkey," said Julie. She straightened the wicker basket on the front. "I want to get one of those Snoopy bike horns for my birthday."

"Your birthday's still a month away," said Ivy.

"Twenty-eight days, to be exact," said Julie. "I can't wait to turn double digits. I'll finally be as old as you." Ivy laughed.

"So, want to ride bikes to Golden Gate Park?" Julie asked. "Mom told me the gardens by the Conservatory have ten thousand tulips and they're all blooming!" The park was just two blocks away.

"Hey, maybe we can get a snow cone, too. I have three dollars left over from my Chinese New Year money," said Ivy.

The girls took off up the hill, their red, white, and blue bike tassels flapping in the wind. They entered the park on a path near the stadium, where picnickers sat on blankets in the grass and teenagers tossed Frisbees. Julie and Ivy swerved when a terrier ran across the path, yipping at their wheels. The girls laughed, speeding toward the Conservatory, a huge greenhouse with an elegant dome like a glass palace. All around it, a sea of purple tulips and yellow daffodils nodded in the spring breeze.

"I've never seen so many flowers," said Ivy. "It smells sweeter than strawberry bubble bath."

"Look at the hummingbird!" said Julie, hopping off

her bike. A green flash of wings zoomed here, there, and back again. The girls sat in the cool grass, people-watching and soaking up the spring sunshine. A guy with a ponytail played a flute, a large hairy dog pulled a kid on roller skates, and a woman in a peasant dress sold crystals to passersby.

"Hold still. Don't move," Ivy whispered. "A butter-fly just landed on your shoulder."

Julie sat as still as stone, moving only her eyes to get a peek. The butterfly had iridescent blue-lavender wings outlined in black.

"Oh my! That's a mission blue butterfly." Julie squinted up to see a white-haired lady smiling back from under the wide brim of a straw hat. Her blue eyes sparkled in a face full of wrinkles. "I couldn't help noticing your new little friend there," said the lady.

"Maybe it thinks you're a flower," said Ivy.

"I've never seen a blue butterfly before," said Julie, watching the butterfly float away.

"That's because they're becoming quite rare. But they love the lupine garden here." The lady nodded toward the tall, showy spikes of purple, pink, and yellow blooms across the path from the tulip garden.

"When I was a girl, we used to go on walks through Muir Woods, and we saw mission blues everywhere. Too bad we don't see more of them nowadays. It was a real treat to see one today." The lady smiled and turned to go. "Nice talking with you girls."

"Bye!" Julie and Ivy called, waving after her as she headed down the pebbled path.

"How about that snow cone?" Julie asked. The girls walked their bikes over to the cart where a vendor called, "Get your snow cones here. Blue raspberry, lemon, lime, watermelon!"

"What can I get for you girls?" he asked, scooping up a ball of crushed ice and filling a paper cone.

"Do we have to pick one flavor?" Julie asked. "Or can we get rainbow?"

"Rainbow it is, coming right up," said the man, squirting red, blue, green, and yellow syrup onto the ball of ice.

"Make that two," said Ivy.

The girls steered their bikes toward a bench under some shade trees, where they slurped their icy treats.

"What's that noise?" Julie asked, looking around.

"That's me slurping," said Ivy.

"No, I mean that little squeak. Hear it?" Both girls craned their necks toward the grove of trees behind their bench.

"There—look," said Julie, jumping up. "I saw something move under that pink bush." The girls stood as still as statues. They did not hear a peep.

"Maybe we scared it," said Julie.

Weep, weep.

Julie looked at Ivy. Ivy looked at Julie. Their eyes grew wide. "There it is again," Julie whispered.

"I heard it, too," Ivy said.

"Sounds like a baby bird," said Julie. The girls peered under the azalea bush. Julie blinked. A pair of round yellow eyes blinked back at her.

"A baby owl!" she whispered. It was no bigger than a tennis ball, with pointy ear tufts and a sharp hooked beak. It was covered with downy gray fuzz as soft as dandelion fluff.

"Where's your mama?" Ivy asked.

"Maybe it's hurt," said Julie. "It must have fallen out of a nest. It's too young to fly." She peered up at the treetops, looking for a nest. "I don't see anything that looks like a nest."

"Even if we did find a nest, how would we get the baby back up into it?" Ivy asked. "And I don't hear a mama owl calling."

"All I hear are those noisy crows," said Julie, glancing at the black birds circling overhead. "They might come after it. We have to save it."

"Can't the mama owl come save it?" Ivy asked.

"What if it's lost? We can't just leave it here—a cat or a dog or a raccoon could find it." Julie untied her sweatshirt from around her waist. She turned it inside out to make a soft bed and set it under the bush next to the owl. "C'mon, little one," she coaxed. "Hop into my sweatshirt and we'll take you home."

The baby bird didn't move.

"Something's wrong with it," said Ivy.

Cupping her hand under the baby owl, Julie lifted it into the soft sweatshirt and eased it out from under the bush. The girls stood a moment, in awe of the small creature.

"Don't be scared," Julie whispered. "We'll take care of you." Carefully, she settled the bird in the basket on the front of her bike. The baby owl nestled down into the folds, as if it were being tucked into bed.

"Aw, he's sooooo cute!" said Ivy. "Look at all that soft, fluffy fuzz."

"Let's get you home, fuzz face," Julie cooed. She hopped on her bike and was just about to push off when she froze. "Wait a minute. We can't take it to my apartment. Pets aren't allowed. You'll have to take it home to your house."

"I can't," said Ivy. "We have two cats, remember? The bird would last about two seconds around Jasmine and Won Ton."

Julie twisted the hem of her shirt, thinking. Ever since her parents' divorce, Julie had been splitting her time between Mom's apartment and Dad's house. She sighed. "I can't take it to Dad's house, since I'm only there on weekends, and he's away a lot."

Ivy grabbed Julie's arm and pointed. "Look, there's that nice lady who told us about the butterflies. Maybe she knows about birds, too."

"Good idea," said Julie. They wheeled their bikes across the grass to the lady, who was bent over sniffing a bright red azalea.

"Excuse me," said Julie.

The woman looked up. "Oh, hello again, girls."

"We found a baby owl," said Julie, parting the folds of her sweatshirt to show the lady. "We heard it crying. We couldn't find its mother or see a nest and we thought we shouldn't leave it there all alone, but we don't know what to do."

"Looks to me like you've found a baby screech owl. They don't build nests—they live in holes in trees."

"No wonder we couldn't see any nest," said Ivy.

"Poor thing's trembling," said the woman. "It must have fallen out of a tree."

"What should we do?" Julie asked.

"It needs help right away," the lady said. "Do you girls know where the Randall Museum is? It's not far from the park. They have a rescue center there. They can take care of injured wild animals."

"It's just a few blocks from my house," said Julie. "I've passed by there lots of times."

"I'm sure they'll know what to do," said the lady.

"Thanks," Julie and Ivy called, hopping back on their bikes. Julie cooed to the little owl all the way out of the park, down Waller Street, and up the hill to the museum.

Feathered Friends

❀ CHAPTER 2 ❀

t the Randall Museum, Julie and Ivy introduced themselves to a young woman with long brown hair who was wearing hiking boots, khaki pants, and a college sweatshirt.

"Hi, I'm Robin Young," she said. "Let's see what you've got there."

Julie held out the sweatshirt nest. She and Ivy told Robin all about finding the baby owl.

"Let's take a look at this little guy." Robin set the bundle down on a table in the workroom. "Looks like a baby screech owl, probably only a week or two old."

"Do you think it's going to be okay?" asked Julie.

"You did the right thing to keep it warm and safe. Most of the time it's best to leave wild creatures alone, but in this case, there's no way this little guy would have made it through the night in the park."

Pulling on gloves, she gently turned the baby owl onto its back.

The owl's head was twitching, and its eyes blinked nonstop.

"Is it scared?" Julie asked.

"Probably." Robin frowned. "Has it been blinking and twitching like this since you found it?"

"Yes," Julie said.

"That's not a good sign," said Robin. "Rapid blinking and head twitching can mean that the bird's been poisoned."

"Who would poison a baby bird?" asked Ivy.

"Nobody poisoned it on purpose. Most likely, it ate something containing pesticides, like DDT."

"What's DDT?" Julie asked.

"A chemical," Robin explained. "Farmers used to spray it on their fields and orchards so that insects wouldn't eat all their crops. Then birds swallowed it when they ate the leaves or insects. A law was passed to stop the use of DDT a few years ago, but we still see the effects of it moving up the food chain."

"Do you think you can save the owl?" Julie asked.

"We'll know in the next forty-eight hours," said

Robin. "For now, I'll get out a heating pad to keep it nice and warm, give it water every fifteen minutes, and see if I can get the little guy to eat a mealworm."

"Can I come back and visit him?" Julie asked.

"Sure, any time," said Robin. "I'm a graduate student at Berkeley, but I'm here most days when I'm not in class."

"Thanks," said Julie. "I'll be back tomorrow."

The next day after school, Julie set off for the museum.

"Hi! Remember me?" she asked Robin.

"Of course," said Robin. "But I'm sorry to say the little owl isn't here. We were afraid it might not make it through the night, so we took it to the vet late yesterday, where it can get around-the-clock care. The vet says the owl made it through the night, so that's a hopeful sign."

"Oh, that's good." But Julie couldn't hide her disappointment at not getting to see the owl again.

"Well, no sense coming here today for nothing," said Robin. "Would you like to meet Shasta and Sierra and their babies?"

"Shasta and Sierra? Are they owls, too?"

"You'll see," said Robin, smiling as if she had a surprise. She led Julie back to a cage the size of a small room. Perched side by side on a large branch were two huge brown eagles with snow-white heads and shiny yellow beaks. Their bright yellow eyes fixed Julie and Robin with a stern gaze.

"Meet Shasta and Sierra, our national symbols," Robin said with a note of pride.

Julie gasped in amazement. She had seen pictures of bald eagles before, but that hadn't prepared her for the sheer size and majesty of these two birds. "I never knew birds could look so intelligent—or so fierce," she whispered.

Robin pointed toward the back of the cage. "See that heap of sticks up on the shelf in back? That's a makeshift nest that we made out of twigs and lined with pine needles. And those two gray fuzzy lumps are Shasta and Sierra's babies."

Julie peered through the wire mesh. Standing on tip-toe, she could just see two downy heads sticking up out of the nest. They looked like speckled balls of lint from the dryer. "They don't look anything like their parents.

They have dark eyes and dark heads," Julie noted.

"They're about four weeks old, still nestlings. They're just starting to get their first feathers."

"Aw," said Julie. "Did they hatch right here at the rescue center?"

"Yep," said Robin. "It was amazing to watch. But we have to keep a close eye on them. Shasta and Sierra are stressed by being in captivity. They're used to hunting and fishing in the wild. They don't always know how to take care of their babies in a confined space."

Julie stood mesmerized. As she watched, one of the adult eagles hopped onto a perch only a few feet away from her.

"That's Shasta," said Robin. "You can tell because the male's a bit smaller than the female."

Up close, Julie saw that Shasta's right wing was bandaged. "What happened to him?" she asked.

"We're not exactly sure," said Robin. "The eagles came to us from Marin County, where trees were being cleared to make room for new houses. We think the tree that held their nest was cut down. Some construction workers found Shasta flapping one wing on the ground, unable to fly. Sierra, his mate, was nearby."

"When his wing heals up, will you be able to let them go?" Julie asked.

"We want to," said Robin. "But the museum doesn't have the funding for an eagle release."

"You mean you can't just let them go outside?"

"No," Robin said with a sigh. "A bald eagle release takes a lot of preparation—and a lot of money. Before we can release them, we need to build a hack tower, and—"

"A hack tower?" Julie asked.

"A platform about forty feet above the ground—as high as an eagle's nest," Robin explained. "It gives the eagles a safe place where they'll have food and shelter for a few months, until they get used to hunting and building nests again in the wild. We'd be working with the Fish and Wildlife Service. They band the eagles and keep track of them and feed them. And somebody has to get paid to do all that."

Julie frowned. "Can't the museum pay to build the tower and everything?"

"It costs at least a thousand dollars, and we just don't have that kind of money. The Randall is a small museum. We run mostly on donations and volunteers,

and we have other animals to care for, too." Robin
shook her head. "The sad part is, if the eagles are in
captivity much longer, it'll be too late—they won't be
able to adapt back to the wild."

"What will happen if they can't go back into the
wild?"

"They'll have to live at a zoo," said Robin.

"Even the baby eagles?" Julie asked.

"We can't let the eaglets go without their parents
to feed them. And one of the babies isn't doing well.
Shasta and Sierra seem confused in this cage, and they
sometimes neglect to feed their babies."

Julie looked into Shasta's intense yellow eyes and
shivered. She could sense the wildness in him. She
couldn't bear the thought of him spending the rest of
his life in a cage.

Endangered

 love driving!" Tracy crowed as she and Julie left the Golden Gate Bridge behind and headed toward the rainbow tunnel. "It was okay driving around the high school parking lot with Dad on Sundays, but it's much more fun having my license."

"Now you can take me everywhere," Julie joked.

"Tell me again why you need me to drive you to the middle of nowhere?" Tracy asked.

"It's a place in Marin County where they're building new houses," said Julie, glancing down again at the paper with the directions Robin had given her. "It's where the bald eagles were found. The builders cut down hundreds of tall trees. It's their fault that Shasta and Sierra are living in a cage now."

When Julie saw a big sign saying Mountain Meadow

Homes, she told Tracy to pull off the highway. A rutted
dirt road led up to a construction trailer. Nervously,
Julie peeked in the open door. A man in jeans, work
boots, and a flannel shirt was bent over blueprints.
"Excuse me," said Julie, stepping inside. "Are you the
man in charge?"

"I'm the foreman," he said, peering over his glasses.
"I'm just guessing you're not the new backhoe operator."

"No, I'm Julie Albright, and this is my sister—"

"—and you're lost."

"No!" said Julie. "I came to talk to you about—about
bald eagles." The foreman raised his eyebrows and
waited for her to continue.

"You're cutting down trees where they have their
nests," she went on.

He rolled his eyes. "Don't tell me you're one of those
tree huggers."

"What's a tree hugger?"

The foreman gave her a thin smile. "Somebody who
cares more about trees than people."

"I care about people," Julie said, standing up straighter.
"But I care about eagles, too. And you're cutting down so
many trees, the eagles have nowhere left to live."

He pinched the bridge of his nose. "Now they're sending me eight-year-olds to pull on the heartstrings."

"For your information, I'm nine, and I'll be ten in a few weeks," Julie replied.

"My mistake. Look, kid, I'm busy. I've got homes to build. And no pipsqueak is gonna shut down this work site."

Julie looked at Tracy, who nudged her, urging her on. She took a deep breath.

"All I know is, because of you, some wild bald eagles have to spend the rest of their lives in a cage unless we get some money to save them. Can't you help?"

"Listen, missy, we had an environmental impact study done before we broke ground on this project. And nobody said one word about any bald eagles. We did our job."

"Don't you even care what happens to the bald eagles? They're our national symbol!"

"And they're endangered," Tracy added. "There are only thirty pairs left in the whole state." Julie smiled gratefully at her sister.

"Look, I'm sorry about the eagles, okay? All I can say is people need homes, too." He gestured out the window toward a cluster of framed-up houses. "A few birds—maybe that's the price of progress."

"Well, you took away their home—it's only fair that your company help them get a new one." Julie explained about the hack tower and the money it cost to release the eagles.

The foreman chewed his pencil for a moment. "Look, tell you what. I'll talk to the boss. Might be we could donate some scrap lumber for that tower of yours. But I'm not making any promises here."

Julie nodded. She scribbled down the phone number of the rescue center and passed it to him. "If your boss says yes, call here and ask for Robin. And thank you!"

"Like I said, no promises, kid."

The next afternoon, Julie bounced into Robin's office. She couldn't wait to tell Robin about the visit to Mountain Meadow Homes. But Robin sat slumped at her desk, her head in her hands.

"Have a seat, Julie," she murmured before Julie had said a word.

Julie sat down, feeling uncertain. Finally Robin

looked up. "We lost one of the baby eagles last night."

Julie hesitated. "Do you want me to help look for it?" she asked.

"Julie," Robin said gently, "the baby eagle died."

"But I just . . . it was . . . how could that happen?" Julie took in a ragged breath, tears beginning to smart.

"We found it this morning, on the floor of the cage," said Robin. "We're not exactly sure what happened. It could have fallen. But I think it has more to do with being in captivity. Shasta and Sierra can't care for their babies the way they would in the wild."

Julie stared at her hands. Her eyes welled with tears.

"I know how you feel," Robin comforted her. "This is the hardest part of my job."

Julie nodded in sympathy. "How's the other baby doing?"

"It's going to need extra care and attention. We'll hand-feed it for a while and monitor it closely."

"Can I see it?" Julie asked.

"Tell you what," said Robin, glancing at her watch. "It's about time for her feeding, and you can help." Robin took a metal bowl out of a large refrigerator.

Julie wrinkled her nose. "Smells fishy."

"That's what it is—fish, chopped into bite-size pieces." Robin took something that looked like an eagle head from a shelf in the workroom. Slipping it over her hand, she made the yellow beak snap open and shut.

Julie's eyes widened. "A bald eagle puppet? It looks just like Shasta and Sierra!"

Robin nodded. "We'll feed the eaglet with this, so that she thinks she's getting food from another eagle. If she imprints to a human, we won't be able to let her go in the wild." Robin put her finger up to her lips. "Watch me first. Then you can take a turn," she whispered.

Julie peered into the nest, which was now in a separate cage. The eaglet looked like a fuzzy ball of lint—tufts of dark gray down with tiny feathers sprouting all over, like white freckles.

With the puppet, Robin scooped up a beakful of fish and reached toward the nest. The baby eagle hungrily snatched the fish scraps out of the puppet's beak. After Robin had fed the eaglet several bites of fish, she whispered, "Want to give it a try?"

Julie nodded, too much in awe to speak. She slipped the bald eagle puppet over her hand, inserting her thumb and fingers into its beak. She scooped up a piece of fish—and dropped it. The baby's dark eyes watched the puppet's every move. Its beak snapped at the bald eagle puppet, looking for food. After a few tries, Julie got the hang of it, and soon the nestling was greedily gulping down every morsel she offered.

Once Julie was comfortable, Robin left her to finish the feeding on her own. Julie felt pleased to be helping. If Shasta and Sierra couldn't take care of their baby, she and Robin would give it extra-special care and attention.

Julie couldn't help thinking about the eaglet that had died. There was nothing she could do to save that one now. But at least she could feed this one, and it would have a fighting chance.

When every last scrap of fish was gone, the scruffy eaglet snuggled down into its nest, fluffing its speckled down.

"Don't you worry—you're gonna make it," Julie whispered. "We're counting on you, Freckles."

Earth Day

On Monday at school, Julie's thoughts kept returning to Shasta, Sierra, and Freckles. She drew a bald eagle flying in the margin of her science notebook. Then she doodled the letters S A V E and filled in the words Save All Vanishing Eagles. It chilled her to think that all over California—all over the country—bald eagles were losing their homes and their lives. Surely if people realized this, they'd stop it from happening.

Julie's teacher, Ms. Hunter, walked to the front of the room and cleared her throat. "Class, who can tell me what special day is coming up?"

Julie's hand shot up. "Earth Day! It's on April twenty-second. And this Saturday, there's going to be a big celebration in Golden Gate Park."

"That's right," said Ms. Hunter. "Now, what can we

do as a class to help planet Earth?"

"We could recycle the used paper from our class-room," said Kimberly.

"Good. What else?" asked Ms. Hunter.

"I saw on TV how fish and ocean birds die from eating plastic trash," said Jeff. "We could pick up litter on the beach."

"Another good suggestion. Any more ideas?"

Julie told the class about the bald eagles at the rescue center. "And it's going to cost at least a thousand dollars to release the eagles back into the wild," she added.

"Helping bald eagles would be cool," said Julie's friend T. J. Everyone agreed and began thinking up ways to raise money—bake sales, car washes, lemonade stands.

Ms. Hunter clapped her hands to quiet the hubbub. "Can we think of a way to not only raise money but also raise awareness about how bald eagles are endan-gered?" she asked.

"There are only thirty nesting pairs of bald eagles left in all of California," Julie told the class. "If people knew that, I'm sure they'd want to help."

"We could launch sixty balloons on Earth Day," said Alison. "One for each bald eagle left in California."

"Wow! Great idea," everybody agreed.

"I think we're onto something here," Ms. Hunter said. "But what happens to all those balloons after they go up?"

"Oh, yeah," said Jeff. "Balloons pop and end up littering."

"How about sixty kites, then?" asked Alison.

"We could fly them on Earth Day all at once and tell everybody what's happening to the bald eagles," Amanda added.

"My mom owns a shop," said Julie. "Maybe she could order some kites."

"How are we going to raise money by flying kites?" Kenneth asked.

The room grew quiet. At last Julie said, "How about if you donate five dollars, you get a kite to fly."

The room buzzed with excitement.

"Class, this sounds like an excellent activity for Earth Day," said Ms. Hunter. "What shall we call our project?"

T. J. reached over and held up Julie's notebook.

"How about Project SAVE, for Save All Vanishing Eagles?"

Ms. Hunter wrote the name in block letters across the blackboard. Looking around the room, Julie felt a surge of pride in her classmates. It was true—people really *did* care about helping the bald eagles. But first they had to know about the problem.

As soon as school let out, Julie raced home. Instead of heading upstairs to the apartment for a snack, as she usually did, she went straight into Gladrags, her mom's shop on the ground floor. When Julie described her class project, Mom agreed to order the kites and donate them to Project SAVE.

"I think I've even seen some kites that have pictures of eagles printed on them," said Mom, handing Julie a catalogue.

Leafing through the catalogue, Julie found the eagle kites. They came in ready-to-assemble kits. Perfect! She couldn't wait to tell Robin.

Suddenly, Julie had another idea. She gave her mom a quick hug, ran upstairs, shoved her tape recorder into her backpack, then hopped onto her bike. If she made it to the rescue center by four o'clock, she'd be there in time to feed Freckles.

Robin's face lit up when Julie told her about Project SAVE. "Kites are a great idea. Why don't we set up an extra table at the Randall Museum's booth and have kids make the kites right there? That would be a great Earth Day activity. And we'll put up a sign thanking Gladrags for donating the kites."

Julie pulled the tape recorder from her backpack. "I was thinking we could play eagle sounds over a loudspeaker at the booth, too. Is it okay for me to tape Shasta and Sierra?"

"That'll sure get everyone's attention," said Robin. "Listen, they're screeching right now."

Kweek kuk kuk, kweek-a-kuk kuk! The harsh cries always gave Julie a thrill of excitement. The calls sounded fierce and wild, just like the eagles. Julie switched her tape player to record and set it outside the eagle cage.

Then it was time to feed Freckles. Julie put on the bald eagle puppet, but when she held out a scrap of fish, Freckles did not snap her beak to take it. In fact, she barely raised her head to look at the puppet.

Julie rushed down the hall to tell Robin.

"That's weird," said Robin. "I haven't fed her since early this morning. She should be hungry."

Robin followed Julie back to the eagle room. "Her eyes look clear," she said, peering at Freckles. "And she has plenty of water, so she shouldn't be dehydrated. She's not shaking or shivering. I don't know what's wrong."

Julie couldn't help thinking of the other baby eagle. "She's not going to die, is she?"

"I hope not," said Robin.

"Maybe she wants to be back in the cage with Shasta and Sierra," said Julie.

"Could be. Sometimes it's hard to figure out what's wrong when birds aren't in their natural environment," said Robin. "I'd better call the vet."

Julie stared helplessly at the little eaglet, willing her to get well. She imagined a day when Freckles, with full-fledged feathers, would soar wild and free high above the treetops. Would that day ever come?

Robin poked her head in. "Julie, your mom just called and wants you home for dinner."

"But Freckles—"

Robin put her hand on Julie's shoulder. "You can't

stay here all night with Freckles. The vet's on his way. You've done all you can do."

"I just don't want to come back tomorrow and find her . . ." Julie couldn't finish her sentence.

Robin shrugged helplessly. "I know, Julie. I know."

Saturday morning, Julie woke to the crunch of a shovel breaking new ground outside her second-story window. Arm-wrestling the window open, she peered down.

Hank, a family friend from the neighborhood, looked up from his digging and waved. He was wearing an owl T-shirt that said *Give a Hoot, Don't Pollute,* and he was smiling under his bushy red beard.

"What are you up to?" Julie asked from her perch.

"We're planting trees along Haight Street for Earth Day," Hank called back. "This one was left over, and I thought it might spruce up the front of Gladrags. It's a red-flowering gum tree." Delicate branches covered with pink blossoms swayed in the light wind. The new tree looked as if it was waving, too.

"It looks great," Julie called. "I'm off to Golden Gate

Park for the big celebration. Happy Earth Day!"

"Have fun!" Hank called back.

Golden Gate Park hummed with activity. The happy rhythm of calypso music pulsed from a stage. Paint-splattered teenagers created a mural splashed with suns and rainbows, whales and ocean waves. Julie made her way down the row of exhibit booths, collecting buttons with slogans like *Save the Whales* and *Every Day Is Earth Day*.

When she found the Randall Museum booth, Robin was setting up a table for the kite-making area. "You're just in time to help me cover this table with paper," said Robin. "Then we'll put out scissors and tape."

"Okay, but first—tell me, what did the vet say today about Freckles?" It had been several days since the vet had taken Freckles in for observation.

"Good news. She's eating again, and we'll probably get her back by Monday. But Dr. Ingram says if we don't get these birds up into the hack tower within the next two weeks, Freckles may never be able to join her parents or live as a wild bird."

Julie swallowed. "Let's hope the kites are a big hit."

"I got this big pickle jar, and I thought we could put it out today for donations," said Robin, setting the jar on the table.

Julie dug deep into her pocket and pulled out a wrinkled bill. "I'm donating the first five dollars. That way the jar won't look so empty."

Soon T. J. and Ms. Hunter showed up to help at the kite-making table. Ivy and her brother, Andrew, were their first customers.

"Five-dollar donation! Make a kite!" T. J. shouted, cupping his hands into a megaphone.

"Save the bald eagles," Julie called out. Soon kids and families crowded around the table, putting their kites together and attaching tails and strings. Julie talked with people of all ages, passing out information and answering questions.

A lady in a straw hat picked up one of the flyers. "Bald eagles!" she said to Julie. "I'm a bird-watcher, and I used to see them from our ranch not so many years ago. But I'm afraid I haven't seen an eagle for quite some time."

"Where's your ranch?" Julie asked curiously.

"Near the coast, in Marin County." The woman looked up from the flyer, and Julie thought she recognized the friendly blue eyes under the wide-brimmed straw hat.

"Hey! Aren't you the butterfly lady?" Julie asked. The woman furrowed her brow. "Remember? That day at the Conservatory—you told me about the blue butterfly that landed on my shoulder."

The lady's blue eyes crinkled with recognition. "So you're the butterfly girl," she said, smiling broadly. "I'm Mrs. Mildred Woodacre. So glad to meet you again."

"I'm Julie Albright," said Julie, and soon the two were chatting like old friends. Julie told her how finding the baby owl that day had led to becoming a volunteer at the rescue center. And she was happy to report that the vet had said the baby screech owl was pulling through.

"What a pretty T-shirt," said Mrs. Woodacre. "Why, it has an eagle on it!"

"My dad got it for me to wear today," Julie said proudly. "Isn't it boss?" She chattered on, telling Mrs. Woodacre the whole story of Shasta, Sierra, and Freckles. "That's why I'm here today," she finished. "We have to raise enough money for the eagles to be released, or they'll live in a cage for the rest of their lives."

"Oh, my," Mrs. Woodacre said softly, putting a hand to her chest. "It just breaks my heart to think of any wild creature living out its life in a cage."

"Hey, Julie," T. J. called. "We've got sixty done—time to launch the kites."

Julie and Ivy picked up the kite they had assembled and made their way over to the grassy meadow not far from the Conservatory. A small crowd of kids and parents gathered atop the hill at the far end of the meadow. Ms. Hunter was helping a group of Julie's classmates get ready to launch their kites.

"Look," said T. J., all out of breath from running. "TV cameras! Ms. Hunter says the KSKY news channel is here for Earth Day. Maybe our kites will be on TV!"

"Then we'd better get them up in the air," said Julie.

"Happy Earth Day," Robin announced. A TV cameraman moved in and pointed the camera right at her, but she did not seem nervous. "Welcome to the Randall Museum's bald eagle kite-flying extravaganza! It's a sad fact that our national symbol, the bald eagle, is rapidly disappearing. Today, thanks to all of you, every kite we send up into the air helps toward the release of three bald eagles at our rescue center." Everybody clapped, and Robin made a final pitch for sending donations to the rescue center. "And now, the girl who helped bring all this about—Julie Albright!"

Taking hold of the microphone, Julie said, "First, I'd like to thank my family, my friends, my teacher, Ms. Hunter, and my whole class at Jack London Elementary School for coming up with this idea and helping to make it happen." Julie's class went wild, whooping and cheering.

A bright light shone on Julie. The camera was pointed at her now. She squinted into the glare, took a deep breath, and said, "Today, sixty eagle kites will fly in the sky—one for each of the bald eagles that have nests in the state of California. With your help, we hope that three real bald eagles will have a chance—a chance to return to the wild, where they belong. Happy Earth Day, everybody. Let's go fly a kite!"

As Julie bent to pick up her kite, a man with a spiral notebook who had been talking to Robin asked, "Julie

Albright? Can I get the correct spelling of your name and your age?"

"Hey," said T. J. excitedly. "Aren't you the weatherman from Channel 12?"

"That's me, Joe Smiley," said the man. "I've been out here all day covering Earth Day."

"Told ya!" said T. J., bouncing on his toes. "Hey, make that foghorn sound you do every morning."

"No, say that thing you always say when it's raining," said Ivy.

"It's raining catfish and frogs out there this morning," said Mr. Smiley in a deep voice. "Better take the boat to work." A bunch of kids gathered around, laughing.

"Is Smiley your real name, Mr. Smiley?" asked another of Julie's classmates.

"Sure is," said the weatherman with a grin.

"Is Julie going to be on TV?" Ivy asked.

"Can't say for sure," said Mr. Smiley. "But we shot a nice clip back there. It just might fit into our Earth Day segment on the six o'clock news." He motioned to the cameraman. "Let's roll!"

Julie and Ivy raced to the top of the grassy hill. Ivy

held the kite high above her head. Holding the reel of string, Julie let out about four feet and with a "Ready, set, go!" took off running down the hill. Ivy let go of the kite, and up, up, up it went. The eagle kite rose on an updraft, high as a tree, until a sudden gust sent it sideways, dipping toward the ground. Julie ran and the kite rose again, catching the strong breeze.

In no time, people of all ages were whooping with delight as their kites lifted off the ground. Julie let out some more string, and her kite soared high, joining the other kites, where they dipped and fluttered, gathering far overhead like a convocation of eagles, white against the blue sky. Julie tilted her head, squinting against the bright rays of the sun until she could see the dark silhouette of the eagle on her kite. Julie imagined it to be Shasta or Sierra, swooping and soaring way up in the sky.

"This is your eagle-eye reporter, Julie Albright, coming to you live from Golden Gate Park." Julie spoke clearly into her ketchup-bottle microphone.

"Shh, here it is," said Tracy, pointing at the television.

Mom, Tracy, and Julie glued their eyes to the six o'clock news on the screen.

Joe Smiley came on. "That's the guy! The one who talked to Robin and me," said Julie. Joe talked about the mayor's Earth Day speech, a mural painted to beautify a playground, and efforts to start curbside recycling in the city. Julie jumped up and pointed. "There's Robin. She's asking for donations to the rescue center."

Just when Julie thought they were going to a commercial break, Joe Smiley said, "One nine-year-old, Julie Albright, is working hard to save our national bird." The camera panned to Julie.

"There you are!" screamed Tracy.

"You're on TV!" said Mom, leaning in closer.

"This young activist believes you can make a difference," said Joe Smiley, pointing his finger at the camera. "To help save the bald eagles, send your donation to the address on the screen."

"Robin will be so happy that they told everybody where to send money," Julie said after the segment ended. "She says we're almost out of time for the eagle release."

"I'm proud of you, honey," said Mom, giving her a sideways squeeze.

Just then the phone rang. Dad had seen Julie on the news, too. They chatted, and then Julie hung up and came back into the living room.

"So, how's it feel to be famous?" Tracy asked.

"I was only on for two seconds," said Julie.

"So? Two seconds of fame is still famous."

"Thanks," said Julie. "But it's the bald eagles that I hope will be famous. Famous for flying free again."

Trying to Fly

⚙ CHAPTER 5 ⚙

On Tuesday after school, Julie biked straight to the rescue center. She thought of the pickle jar chock-full of coins and dollar bills on Earth Day. The bald eagles had even been mentioned on TV! *Shasta and Sierra will surely be released now,* thought Julie.

Julie poked her head into Robin's office. "So, are we going to get that hack tower built?"

Robin looked up and smiled, but she didn't have the upbeat expression that Julie was expecting. "I've counted the money twice," said Robin. "We raised three hundred dollars from the kites, and another forty-two dollars from the donations in the pickle jar. But we still come up way short."

Julie frowned, doing the math in her head. "To reach a thousand dollars, we need another . . . six hundred fifty-eight dollars." She paused, sobered by the large number. "Well, now that it's been on the news, I bet people will send in all kinds of money."

"We have had a few donations already," said Robin, "but only small amounts so far—nothing like what we need. If we don't have the money by Friday, Fish and Wildlife can't start building the tower next week. And we just can't wait any longer."

"But—" Julie scuffed the leg of the table with the toe of her shoe.

"I'm sorry, Julie. After all your hard work, I know this isn't what you wanted to hear."

"Shasta and Sierra can't go to a zoo now," said Julie. "It's just not right."

Robin sighed. "Listen, would you do me a big favor and feed Freckles? That always cheers you up."

Julie nodded and headed down the hall. Freckles needed her, and that's what she had to fix her mind on for the moment.

Freckles was feisty and growing bigger by the day. Hungrier than usual, she gulped down the fish in no time. Julie was just washing off the eagle puppet when she heard a voice call out, "Yoo-hoo! Anybody

here?" Julie hurried out of the workroom and saw
a white-haired woman in a familiar straw hat.

"Mrs. Woodacre! Hi," Julie said. "Are you here to
see Shasta and Sierra?"

"I most certainly am," said Mrs. Woodacre. "After
hearing about your bald eagles on Earth Day, I had to
come and see them for myself."

"I'll be your tour guide." Julie motioned for Mrs.
Woodacre to follow her.

Julie stopped in front of the big cage. The two
huge eagles sat motionless on their perches, fixing
their audience with the fierce gaze that always gave
Julie the shivers. She and Mrs. Woodacre watched in
humbled silence.

"Aren't they amazing?" Julie whispered.

"Magnificent," Mrs. Woodacre said softly.

In the blink of an eye, Shasta threw back his head
and let out a piercing screech. Hopping off his perch,
he lifted into the air, beating his wings furiously, then
glided to the floor.

"Whoa—he flew!" Julie gasped.

"He must be testing his wings," said Mrs. Woodacre.

"I bet his injured wing is all healed now. Let's go

tell Robin he's trying to fly."

"That was quite a show!" said Mrs. Woodacre as they returned to the front office. "Now, I can't leave without one of those eagle kites. I'm going to fly it at the ranch when my grandson comes to visit."

"We have a few extras left over from Earth Day," said Julie. "I'll go get one."

While Mrs. Woodacre chatted with Robin about the eagles, Julie riffled through the boxes from Earth Day. "Here," said Julie, handing a kite kit to Mrs. Woodacre. "All you need are tape and scissors. It's pretty easy."

"Sounds fine," said Mrs. Woodacre.

"And, uh—we're asking five dollars for the kites," Julie added awkwardly.

"Well, then, good thing I brought my checkbook today," Mrs. Woodacre said with a wink. Unsnapping her pocketbook, she filled out a check and handed it to Julie.

"Thanks," said Julie. "I hope you have fun flying kites with your grandson." She started to hand the check to Robin, then stopped. Something wasn't right.

"I think you made a mistake," she said slowly.

"There are too many zeros."

"No mistake," said Mrs. Woodacre, smiling.

Julie took in a breath. "Five hundred dollars! For real?" She clutched the check to her chest.

"Bald eagles were a part of my childhood," said Mrs. Woodacre. "I hope they'll be around for generations."

"I can't tell you how much we appreciate this," said Robin, shaking Mrs. Woodacre's hand. "We were hundreds of dollars short for the eagle release, but now ... thank you!"

After Mrs. Woodacre left, Julie turned to Robin. "Does this mean ..." she began, almost afraid to hope.

Robin bit her lip. "We're so close now, but—" Suddenly she smacked her fist into her palm, as if she'd reached a decision. "I'm going to call Fish and Wildlife right now and see if they'll give us the go-ahead even though we're still a hundred fifty dollars short." Just as Robin reached for the phone, it rang.

"Randall Museum rescue center," she said, picking it up. "Yes, this is Robin Young . . . Who? You have what? Scrap lumber? Oh ... Yes, that young lady was right. We do need to build a tower ... Yes! We'll take it, definitely. Thanks so much!"

Robin hung up the phone and gave Julie a stunned look. Then she held out her arms and picked Julie right up off the ground in a big bear hug.

Happy Birthday, Julie!

❀ CHAPTER 6 ❀

You Are Invited
Come celebrate
Julie's 10th Birthday
and watch the bald
eagle release!

WHO: Julie Albright with Shasta,
   Sierra, and Freckles

WHAT: Bald Eagle Birthday
   Beach Party

WHERE: Muir Beach

WHEN: May 1, 1976 -12 p.m.

B.Y.O.B.B.
(Bring Your Own Beach Blanket)

Using her best cursive, Julie finished filling out the last of her party invitations. She double-checked her list:

Mom
Dad
Tracy
Ivy
J. J.
Robin
Mrs. Woodacre

Good, she had made seven invitations. Julie left two on the kitchen table for Mom and Tracy and then headed outside.

At the rescue center, Julie leaned in the doorway, looking all around. In just a month it had become like a second home to her. And now Robin and the eagles were going to be part of her birthday—the most important part.

Julie's heart skipped a beat, imagining the moment, less than a week away. For days, Shasta had been testing his wings every chance he got.

"Do you think Shasta's ready to fly?" Julie asked

Robin as she handed her an invitation.

Robin nodded. "He's ready."

"Will the hack tower be built in time?"

"Don't you worry, birthday girl," said Robin. "Fish and Wildlife has a crew already working on it. They'll have it up before the weekend. That gives us a few days to get the eagles used to their new home before we open the door and let them fly."

"But what about Freckles? Will Shasta and Sierra know what to do once they're back in the wild?"

"That's the sixty-four-thousand-dollar question. There's a lot we don't know about releasing eagles. We won't be able to hand-feed Freckles anymore, but we'll make sure she has enough food until Shasta and Sierra start hunting again."

"I can't wait," said Julie. "I feel like I could fly!"

The San Francisco Bay sparkled as Julie and her family crossed the Golden Gate Bridge. She rolled the window down, letting the wind whip her hair. "Happy birthday, world," Julie called out the window.

"I can't believe my little girl's turning ten years old,"

said Mom as they turned off the highway and headed toward the beach on California Route One.

"Yeah! Double digits!" said Julie.

They threaded their way up and over Mount Tamalpais on a ribbon of road that wound its way through lofty redwood trees toward the coast.

"We're here!" Julie shouted, scrambling to be first out of the car.

"Wait up!" yelled Tracy. "Just 'cause it's your birthday doesn't mean you don't have to help carry stuff."

Arms full, they made their way down a path edged with wild purple lupine and fiery Indian paintbrush. Julie and Ivy ripped off their shoes and ran to the water's edge, daring to stick their toes in the icy-cold Pacific. They squealed in delight as ocean waves crashed up over their ankles.

Soon Dad and the others were arriving, and introductions were made all around. Tracy helped Dad build a campfire, while Mrs. Woodacre helped Mom set out the food. Julie and T. J. tossed a Frisbee, starting a game of keep-away from Robin and Ivy. Before long, everybody was feasting on chicken kebabs and potato salad and sipping lemonade.

When the picnic was over, Dad handed Julie a present. "I know we said we'd wait to open presents back at home, but I have one that couldn't wait. You'll see why."

Julie tore off the wrapping. "Binoculars!"

"Happy birthday, honey," said Dad.

"Thanks," Julie said, throwing her arms around him. "It's almost time," she exclaimed, looking up at the hack tower through her binoculars.

Robin checked her watch. "The guys from Fish and Wildlife said they'll open the cage at two o'clock. But that doesn't mean the eagles will fly as soon as the door is opened. So don't get your hopes up too high."

"Too late for that," said Tracy. "Julie's hopes are already sky-high." Everyone laughed.

"Will the baby eagle fly, too?" T. J. asked.

"Freckles isn't old enough to fly yet," Robin explained. "She's only about eight weeks old. In a few more weeks, when she's fully fledged out, she'll be able to leave the tower, too."

Julie passed around her binoculars, and the others took turns getting the hack tower into view.

"I see them!" said Ivy. "One of the big eagles is

flapping all around inside the tower."

"Let me see," said Julie, peering through the binoculars. "That's Sierra. You can always tell the female because she's bigger than the male. And hey, it looks as if she's preening Freckles."

At two o'clock, a hush fell over the gathering. Everyone waited, heads tilted back, eyes glued to the spot at the top of the headland cliffs. Julie held her breath. The only sound was the crashing of the waves.

"Nothing's happening," she said impatiently. "Dad, what time is it?"

"It's only been ten minutes," said Dad.

"Feels like an hour," said T. J.

"Feels like forever," said Julie.

"We have to be patient," said Robin. "Remember, they may not even fly today at all."

After a while, Mom started packing up the picnic basket.

"Maybe they're just not ready yet," said Dad. "Even pilots have days they don't feel like flying," he joked, with a wink at Julie.

But Julie was too anxious to smile back. "Ten more minutes," she pleaded. She picked up the binoculars and pointed them at the hack tower one more time. "Wait—I think I see something moving. It's Sierra. She came out! She just hopped onto the perch pole on the tower."

"And there's Shasta, right behind her," said Ivy, who was looking through Dad's field glasses.

The two eagles flapped and jumped, and then rose up off the platform and perched on top of the hack tower. Mom and Mrs. Woodacre clapped.

"C'mon, Shasta. C'mon, Sierra," T. J. called. "You can do it."

"Fly!" Julie cried. "Fly!"

Suddenly there was a great flapping of wings and several loud screeches. *Kree! Kree!* Sierra launched off the perch pole, circled the tower once, and landed on the branch of a windswept cypress tree. *Krr-eee! Krr-eee!* Sierra called. Shasta leapt off the tower to join her, swooping and gliding, and landed next to his mate.

The two birds lingered a moment. Then, in a whoosh of wings, they flew back in unison and perched again on the hack tower.

"They did it—they flew!" said Julie, jumping up and down.

"That short test flight is probably it for now," said Robin. "Especially with Shasta's injured wing."

"Maybe they need more practice," said Julie. "Practice being free."

Before she could say another word, Shasta glided off the hack tower, out into open space, out over the beach beyond the cliff. Julie and the others watched silently, breathlessly. Even without binoculars he was clearly visible, a speck high above, looping gracefully across the sky.

Suddenly, without warning, Shasta began tumbling in a tailspin toward the ground.

"Nooooo!" Julie shouted, waving her arms and running down the beach. Sierra flew out and hovered in the air above her mate, screeching and calling to Shasta.

Halfway down the beach, Julie stood frozen, watching the drama unfold. She could not take her eyes off Shasta as he spiraled toward the ground. *Fly, Shasta, fly,* she pleaded in silent prayer. She raised outstretched hands. If only she could break his fall, lift him back up on the wind.

Just when she could hardly bear to watch, a strong gust filled Shasta's wings, lifting him up and up.

A chorus of cheers and hoorays resounded from below. Julie raced back to her friends and family, sand flying. "He did it. He's going to make it!" She trained her binoculars back on the hack tower. "Hey, Freckles hopped over to the doorway. She's watching, too."

Shasta had joined Sierra now. As Julie watched in silent admiration, the eagle pair took wing out over the ocean, soaring on the wind.

Flying

As spring passed into summer, Julie thought often about the eagles. She wondered if Shasta's broken wing had healed up as good as new, and if Freckles had learned to fly yet. She especially liked to imagine the three bald eagles soaring high in the sky. Flying was often on Julie's mind, because shortly after school let out in mid-June, Dad had informed her that she was going to fly for the first time—on an airplane!

Julie lifted her long calico dress to lace up her shoes, smoothed her apron, and tied the strings of her sunbonnet. "How do I look?"

"Like a real pioneer," said Mom, taking straight pins from between her lips. "I have to finish off this hem. Dad'll be here to pick you girls up first thing in the morning."

❧ Flying ❧

As Mom pinned up the hem of the pioneer dress, Julie hugged herself with excitement. Tomorrow Dad was taking Tracy and her to the airport for their very first trip on an airplane. They were flying east to Pittsburgh, where Julie and Tracy would join their Aunt Catherine, Uncle Buddy, and cousins Jimmy and April to celebrate the Fourth of July.

But this was not just any July Fourth celebration, Julie reminded herself. It was the Bicentennial, and Julie and her sister were going to be part of a very special event. An old-fashioned pioneer-style wagon train, with wagons from all fifty states, was crossing the country in honor of America's two-hundredth birthday. Except unlike in the pioneer days, this wagon train was starting on the West Coast and heading east, all the way to Pennsylvania. "It's like history in reverse," Dad had put it. In Pittsburgh, Julie and Tracy would join their cousins on a horse-drawn wagon for the last three weeks of the journey.

Julie shivered with anticipation. An airplane . . . and a covered wagon! She would be like Laura Ingalls Wilder, who had crossed the prairie with her family in the Little House books. Julie could hardly wait.

Tracy stopped brushing her hair and held up the green and white cotton dress Mom had made for her. "Did pioneers really wear these long dresses and ugly aprons? I'll die of embarrassment if I have to wear this. I look like Raggedy Ann."

"You can wear blue jeans on the wagon," said Mom. "But take the dress—you may want to wear it when you get to Valley Forge."

"Think of it as dressing up for a big giant birthday party for our whole country," Julie said with enthusiasm. "Just think, two hundred years ago was the original Fourth of July, with the Declaration of Independence." Julie held up a hairbrush in a dramatic pose. "Give me liberty or give me death!"

"Give me my hairbrush," said Tracy, grabbing the brush and stuffing it into her overflowing suitcase. "Okay, I'll take the dress, but I need a second suitcase. I haven't even packed my pillow yet, or my magazines, or—"

"Why not take your tennis racket, and your hair dryer, and your princess phone?" Julie asked, turning to admire her pioneer outfit in the mirror.

"Ha, ha, Julie Ingalls Wilder," Tracy teased back.

Mom smiled. "I sure am going to miss you girls," she sighed, handing each of them a gift.

Julie unwrapped her present. Inside was a blank book covered in fabric with orange pop-art daisies. "A journal!" She hugged the book to her. "Thanks, Mom. It's perfect."

"A trip like this is a once-in-a-lifetime event," said Mom. "You'll want to remember everything that happens."

Julie finished packing. It didn't take long—from all the weekends she'd spent at Dad's house, she'd become an expert packer. She neatly tucked her pioneer dress on top of her jeans, her T-shirts, and her Little House books.

"Please tell me you're not taking all nine of those books in your suitcase," said Tracy.

"Why not? At least my stuff all fits in one suitcase." Julie glanced at Tracy's two bulging suitcases. "Looks like you're taking your whole closet and half the bath-room."

Tracy shrugged. "So? Anything could happen on this trip. This way I'll be prepared no matter what."

That night, a fluttery mixture of excitement and nervousness kept Julie from falling asleep. She opened her new journal to the first page and wrote:

Things I want to do on my trip:

Ride a horse
Learn pioneer stuff like building a fire
Sleep in a tent
Make friends with cousin April

Julie paused and chewed the end of her pencil. There was something else she wanted to add, but she didn't know quite how to put it. Finally she wrote:

Do something special for my country.

She read over her list. The last line looked a little funny. After all, the wagon train was something special. Maybe that was enough. But Julie couldn't help hoping that somehow she could do more than just go along for the ride. She thought back to Earth Day, when she had helped raise money for the eagles' release. Watching those eagles finally soaring free had been more thrilling than any fireworks on the Fourth of July. Just thinking about it made Julie shiver with happiness.

The wagon train journey would be a once-in-a-lifetime event, as Mom had said. Julie hoped that somehow, she could be a special part of it.

"Buckle up," said Julie's father. "We're getting ready for takeoff."

Julie looked out the window as the 707 pulled away from the terminal. "This is so boss! Is it hard to drive one of these things, Dad?"

"Not if you know how." Julie's father smiled. "If you think this is fun, just wait until we're twenty-seven thousand feet above the earth."

Julie looked at her sister with excitement, but Tracy sat stiffly, facing forward and gripping the armrests of her seat.

"Just relax, honey. Flying's even safer than riding

in a car," Dad reassured her.

"But in a car, the wheels never leave the ground," Tracy muttered. As the plane started to taxi down the runway, picking up speed, she reached over and gripped Dad's hand.

"Close your eyes," Dad softly encouraged. "Take a deep breath."

Soon they were high up in the air. The sky was the brightest blue Julie had ever seen, and the plane hovered over pillows of cotton-candy clouds. "Tracy, look! I can see the Golden Gate Bridge. And there are teeny little cars that look like toys."

Tracy glanced out the window and then sank back in her seat, looking a bit green. But her face lit up when Dad handed her a set of headphones and showed her how to tune in the music channels.

Dad took out a map of Pennsylvania and spread it across Julie's tray table. Julie traced her finger along the route Dad had highlighted. It ended at Valley Forge.

"Dad, how come all the wagons are going to Valley Forge?" Julie asked.

"Well, it's a big park, so there'll be enough space for

all the wagons, horses, and people," said Dad. "And two hundred years ago, George Washington and his soldiers spent a long, hard winter in Valley Forge during the Revolutionary War. So it's an important place in history."

"Yeah, they were freezing and starving," Tracy chimed in. "We read about it in school. They didn't have enough shoes, or coats, or food, or anything. A lot of soldiers got sick." She shook her head. "I never would have made it, that's for sure."

Dad chuckled. "Even those soldiers barely made it, but in the end, they pulled through—and turned the tide of the war. And because of them, we're here today, and our country is two hundred years old."

Julie thought back to that winter so long ago. It was difficult imagining the hardships those soldiers had lived through—and all because they had this idea of starting a new country. Would she be willing to go through that, all for an idea that might not even work? And later, settlers crossing the country in horse-drawn wagons to find new homes had known hunger and sickness, too. Julie looked out the airplane window into the vast blue sky. It was strange to think about George Washington and his soldiers, pioneers like Laura Ingalls and her family, and now her own family flying through the air in a jet plane—and how they were all part of the same country. They were all connected.

Wagons, Ho!

❁ CHAPTER 8 ❁

It was still dark the next morning when Julie, Tracy, and Dad headed out of the city to meet their cousins at the crack of dawn. They crossed a long bridge, leaving the glittering lights of Pittsburgh behind them.

"No more cities for a while," Dad said. "From now on, it'll be back roads, farmland, and mountains."

"Do you think April will like me?" Julie could barely remember her cousin, whom she hadn't seen since she was five. "I wonder if she likes the Little House books. Do you think she'll have a pioneer dress, too?" Or would April think it was embarrassing, the way Tracy did?

"I think she'll like you much better if you're not such a Chatty Cathy at five o'clock in the morning," Tracy grumbled. Chatty Cathy was a doll that talked

and talked when you pulled her string. Julie knew
Tracy was teasing her. But she couldn't help smiling,
knowing that Tracy would have to get up early *every*
morning on the wagon train!

❀

As the sun rose, Julie climbed out of the car near
the boat dock and gazed at the strange flotilla slicing
through the early morning fog on the river. A tugboat
pushing two long barges headed toward the dock.
Each barge carried rows of pioneer-style wagons with
big white canvas covers. In a silent parade, the wagons
came to shore. Throngs of people had gathered at the
dock and teams of horses stood patiently, waiting to be
hitched up.

"Julie! Tracy! Uncle Dan! Over here!" A long-legged
girl with brown hair, bangs, and dimples waved her
arms. "It's me, April!" Behind her, Julie recognized
Aunt Catherine, Uncle Buddy, and her cousin Jimmy.
They all hurried over, engulfing Julie, Tracy, and Dad
in a sea of hugs.

Dad stepped back and took a good look at his
niece and nephew. "April, I can't believe you're already

thirteen. And look at those sideburns on Jimmy."
Jimmy grinned, blushing pink to the roots of his
collar-length, wavy brown hair. He was eighteen.

"Don't you think he looks kind of like Pa from *Little
House on the Prairie*?" asked April. "That's my all-time
favorite TV show."

"Hey, those are my favorite books!" said Julie.

"She brought the whole set with her." Tracy rolled
her eyes.

"That's why I can't wait to ride in a real covered
wagon," Julie said. "Sometimes Laura used to ride
the wagon horses to get water. Do you think I can
try riding a horse?"

"You've never ridden a horse before?" April said,
sounding surprised. "Wait till you meet Jimmy's horse,
Hurricane."

It was Julie's turn to be surprised. She looked at
Jimmy. "You have your own horse?"

Jimmy nodded proudly. "Took me four years to
save up for him."

"April's a good rider, too," said Aunt Catherine.
"I'm sure she'd be happy to teach you to ride, Julie."

"I'm off to get my instructions," Jimmy announced.

"See you all at camp tonight!"

"Jimmy volunteered to be one of the outriders,"
Uncle Buddy told them. "They make sure the cars
don't interfere with the horses on the road, things
like that." As Jimmy headed off, he stopped to shake
hands with a man dressed in overalls. "Hey, there's
Tom Sweeney," said Uncle Buddy. "Tom! Come say
hello," he called. "We have two newcomers joining
our wagon."

"Mr. Sweeney's our neighbor—he owns the farm
next to ours," Aunt Catherine explained. "He's the
history buff who got us going on this trip. It's his
wagon and horses we're using."

Mr. Sweeney came over and shook hands with Dad,
Julie, and Tracy. "So you're the city folks. Pleased to
have you join us on the trail," said Mr. Sweeney, flashing a bright smile from within a tanned, leathery face.

"It's my girls who are joining you," Dad said. "I'm
just here to see them off."

"In that case, have you signed the rededication
pledge yet?" Mr. Sweeney unrolled a long piece of
paper. Across the top, in fancy calligraphy, it read
"Pledge of Rededication." Below was a quote from

the Declaration of Independence, with columns of blank lines for signatures.

"By signing this pledge, people are saying they still believe in the principles our country was founded on—freedom and equality, just like it says in the Declaration of Independence," said Mr. Sweeney. "Millions of people have already signed, and we're collecting the signed scrolls as we roll across the country. At Valley Forge we'll present them to the president. He'll sign one, too."

"*The* president?" asked Tracy. "As in President Ford?"

Mr. Sweeney grinned. "That's the one."

Dad gave a low whistle. "You girls may get to see the president," he said.

Mr. Sweeney went on. "At every town we stop in, people bring us signed scrolls to take to Valley Forge. Would you girls like to help me collect them?"

Julie and April nodded. "I know how to collect signatures," said Julie. "I had my own petition for our school basketball team."

"Great. I'll be glad to have more help," said Mr. Sweeney. "Now, go ahead and sign your own names, if you like." He held out the scroll and offered Dad a pen.

Dad and Tracy signed their names and passed the scroll to Julie. The fancy writing at the top made the scroll look very important. Under the title it said:

To commemorate this nation's Bicentennial we hereby dedicate ourselves anew to the precepts of our Founding Fathers: We hold these truths to be self-evident, that all men are created equal . . .

Julie wrote her name on the scroll, using her best cursive. It gave her a chill to sign her name to the pledge, along with millions of other Americans. *I'm making history,* she thought.

At the dock, the wagons were being rolled off the barges one by one. A short, stocky man wearing a badge announced, "Alaska!" as the first official state wagon rolled down the ramp. A hearty cheer rang through the crowd as each wagon was eased off the barge.

"That's Mr. Wescott, the wagon master," April told Julie. "Come on, let's go see our wagon." She led Julie over to her parents, who were harnessing two heavy brown workhorses.

Uncle Buddy looked up. "Meet Mack and Molly,

two of the finest Belgian draft horses in Pennsylvania."

Julie held out a hand to Molly, who nuzzled her with a soft snuffle. Suddenly Molly lifted her head, ears pricked forward, and Julie heard thundering hoofbeats. Looking up, she saw Jimmy riding high atop a tall brown and white paint. Julie backed up as the paint sniffed noses with Mack and Molly and then squealed, tossing his head and prancing sideways. Julie didn't know if it was Hurricane's sheer size or his energy that startled her more. Sucking in a short breath, she could feel the drumbeat of her own heart pounding inside her chest.

"Easy, boy," said Aunt Catherine, reaching up to stroke Hurricane's head and neck. She winked at Julie. "He knows he's a beauty."

Julie smiled thinly. She'd been counting the days till she could ride a horse, but now, at the thought of getting on such a mountain of a creature, her knees weakened.

"Don't mind him," said Jimmy, motioning to Julie to come closer. "He's just excited. Go ahead, you can pet him."

Nervously, Julie reached up to pet the horse on the

neck. Hurricane let out a low nicker, and Julie snatched back her hand.

Jimmy chuckled. "That means he likes you."

Suddenly the wagon master's voice rose above the hubbub. "Wagons, ho!" he called. "Load 'em up and moooooove 'em out!"

"Time to go," called Uncle Buddy, buckling one of Mack's harness straps.

"Have a great time," said Dad, hugging his daughters good-bye.

"I wish you were coming too, Dad," Julie said as she and Tracy hugged him back.

"I know, honey. I can't take the time off. But I'll fly the Philadelphia route so that I can meet up with you for the Fourth of July." Dad helped Julie and Tracy up into the wagon.

The wagon had new paint and a warm barn smell. It was crammed full of suitcases, sleeping bags, blankets, food, camping gear, a toolbox, and a bucket of horse brushes. Julie and April accidentally elbowed each other and then broke into giggles as Julie made her way back to sit down on top of a blanket.

"I can barely stand up in here," said Tracy,

touching the inside of the white canvas cover with her hand. "This whole wagon's not much bigger than my canopy bed at home!"

"It reminds me of being inside forts that Jimmy and I used to make with blankets over the kitchen table," April said.

"I think it's cozy," said Julie.

Soon the wagon wheels were creaking and rolling out of the park and onto the dusty road. The girls waved to Dad as he became smaller and smaller, framed by the horseshoe-shaped opening in the canvas at the back of the wagon

"See you at Valley Forge," Julie called.

Mile after mile, farm after farm, hill after hill, the wagons rolled along past farmhouses, barns, and fields of grazing cows. Perched on a cooler, Julie could see the whole wagon train stretched out behind her like beads on a necklace, disappearing around a curve in the road. There was so much to look at—horses with fancy harnesses and bells on, colorful flags flapping, men in buckskin outfits and Daniel Boone caps, even a dressed-up couple in a wagon that said *Just Married*. Bringing up the rear was an old green station wagon with an American flag on its antenna.

Soon Julie noticed that she could feel every rock and rut in the road under the wagon's wooden wheels. "It's so bumpy, I think my bones are being rearranged," she remarked.

April nodded. "You get used to it after a while."

"In a few days, I bet you'll forget what it's like to ride in a car," Uncle Buddy joked.

At last it was time to stop for lunch. The wagons pulled off the road into a park outside a small town. Children who had been playing in the park gathered nearby, pointing and watching with wide eyes. April nudged Julie as they climbed out of the wagon, saying, "I bet those kids wish they were riding with us!" Julie nodded, proud to be part of such an unusual and important happening.

"I'm so hungry, I could eat a horse," said Uncle Buddy as Aunt Catherine passed out sandwiches.

"Don't say that, Dad—Mack and Molly can hear you!" April laughed.

Julie lay back on the picnic blanket, relieved to have

a rest from the bumpy wagon. "This is the best tuna sandwich I've ever had," she announced.

Aunt Catherine smiled. "Food always tastes better on the trail."

A short, stocky man approached. From his badge, Julie recognized him as the wagon master. He shook hands with Uncle Buddy. "Tom Sweeney tells me you have two new wagoneers," he said.

Uncle Buddy introduced Julie and Tracy. "This is Mr. Wescott, our wagon master. He rides in the official Pennsylvania state wagon and leads the way. He's the boss, so make sure you listen to him!" Mr. Wescott winked at the girls.

"I can tell them the rules," said April. "Stay together. Safety first, especially when cars are on the road. And no making money by selling wagon-train souvenirs to people along the way."

Mr. Wescott let out a hearty laugh. "Couldn't have said it better myself. We should make you assistant wagon master. Speaking of souvenirs, I've got to go talk to that fellow." He nodded in the direction of the station wagon with the flag. "He's got a carload of knick-knacks. Some of these folks are becoming quite a nuisance—looking for any way to make a buck, I guess." Waving good-bye, the wagon master headed off.

"That car's been following the wagon train all day," said Jimmy.

Uncle Buddy nodded. "It's a free country, so Mr. Wescott can't stop that fellow from using the roads. All he can do is ban him from selling souvenirs from the wagon train itself."

Julie munched on an apple. "When do we get to help collect scrolls?" she asked.

"In Bakersville, in a few days," said Aunt Catherine. "But right now, you can help me collect paper plates and apple cores."

"Come on, let's go feed the apple cores to Mack and Molly," said April.

❁

When the wagon train finally made camp that night, Julie was so tired, she could barely help April and Tracy pitch the tent they were going to share. But before she turned off her flashlight and went to sleep, she opened her journal and began to write.

June 15

First day on the wagon train. It seemed like we covered a lot of ground, but Jimmy says we went only four miles!

After lunch, I walked right up to Hurricane and fed him an apple core. I don't want April to know I'm a little scared of him. I still want to ride him (I think). Maybe tomorrow.

Tonight Uncle Buddy got out his banjo, and pretty soon we had a fiddle player, two guitars, and a white-haired lady on dulcimer around our campfire. We sang along to "Oh, Susannah" and "She'll Be Comin' Round the Mountain" and ended up laughing more than singing. I felt just like Laura when Pa used to play his fiddle!

Gotta go. April is trying to spy on me and see what I'm writing. I'll get her back—by tickling her to death when she least expects it!

Lightning Kelley

CHAPTER 9

June 18

More wagons join us every day. This morning April and I counted forty-one wagons in our wagon train. Around noon we arrived in the town of Bakersville. The high school marching band led us through the town, and hundreds of people lined the streets to cheer us on. It was sort of a parade. My arm aches from waving so much!

At lunch, we sat near the bandstand in the town square, where the lady mayor held a special scroll-signing ceremony. She talked about how her grandmother got her start when she came from Ireland at the turn of the century and worked in a cigar factory, making only about five dollars a week. She saved every penny and one day opened her own bakery, and it's still there today.

Then Mr. Sweeney held the scroll as she signed it. When

she handed it back to him, I could see tears shining in her
eyes. It gave me goose bumps.

As the days passed, Julie settled into the rhythm
of life on a wagon train. Each morning, Aunt Catherine
made oatmeal and hot chocolate for breakfast. After
breakfast, Julie packed up her bedding and helped
April and Tracy take down their small tent. While
Uncle Buddy harnessed Mack and Molly, the girls
helped Aunt Catherine load the wagon. Then they all
climbed aboard, waving good-bye to Jimmy as he rode
off to join the outriders, and took their place in the line
of wagons moving slowly out onto the road.

The June weather was fine and sunny, with a
welcome breeze that kept the horses from overheat-
ing. The girls usually started out riding with their legs
hanging out the back, watching the scenery go by.
Sometimes they took turns riding up in front on the
buckboard seat with April's parents or walked alongside the wagon to stretch their legs. One afternoon a
thunderstorm blew up. The sky darkened, and Aunt
Catherine quickly drew the canvas cover closed at

both ends. The three girls sat cozily on the floor of the wagon, listening to the rain patter on the canvas cover and giggling about everything and nothing. Julie had never heard anyone laugh as much as her cousin April! Just hearing April giggle made Julie crack up, even when she had no idea what the joke was. And the girls didn't mind the rain. It gave them a chance to play cards and board games and Twenty Questions. The hours slipped by in a rhythm as steady as Mack's and Molly's hoofbeats.

At midday the wagon train usually stopped in a park or field where the horses could graze. While Tracy helped Aunt Catherine prepare lunch, Julie and April liked to wander among the wagons, saying hello to the other people and horses, and each trying to be the first to spot Jimmy and Hurricane. One day they found Jimmy hunched over his saddle, fixing a stirrup strap. Hurricane was tied to a nearby tree.

Jimmy looked up as the girls approached. "April, would you mind taking Hurricane down to the stream for a drink? He's cooled off now." Jimmy had warned Julie that you couldn't water a horse that was still hot and sweaty—the horse could get sick.

April nodded. "Sure. C'mon, Julie." She untied Hurricane's rope and started across the field toward the creek. Suddenly she turned to Julie. "Hey, want to ride Hurricane? I'll boost you up."

"Really?" Julie's heart began to pound. "But wait. What about a saddle?"

"You can ride bareback," said April. "It's super fun. C'mon, I'll give you a leg up." She cupped her hands to make a foothold. Julie stepped into April's hand and, in one swift motion, swung her other leg up and over the horse.

"Hold on to his mane," April instructed. As April led Hurricane across the grassy field, Julie wobbled from side to side. Hurricane's bare back was slippery. She hunkered down low, clinging to the horse's mane.

"Try to relax," April coached. "Sit up straight and get your balance."

Gradually Julie sat up a little taller, gripping the sides of the horse with her thighs. She eased into the rocking motion of the horse, feeling his warmth against her legs, his back muscles rippling with each step.

"Good—that's it. You're getting it," said April.

"I'm really riding!" said Julie.

"You're doing great! Want to try a trot?" April asked.

"Sure, why not," said Julie.

"Here, take the rope." April tossed the end of the lead rope up to her. Julie let go of the mane with one hand and caught it.

"Now kick him with your heels," April called. She broke into a jog. "Let's go, Hurricane."

Julie swung out her feet and gave the horse a kick. Hurricane shot across the field, heading straight for the creek. *Ba-da-rump, ba-da-rump, ba-da-rump.* All Julie could hear was the beating of hooves and the whoosh of air in her ears. "Help!" she called, but April was fast falling behind.

"Hangggg onnn!" April's voice was nearly lost in the thundering of hooves.

Julie clung desperately to Hurricane's side, one leg barely hooked over his back. She clutched at his mane. All she could see was the ground—and Hurricane's pounding hooves. Dust stung her eyes. Her heart thumped against her rib cage. If she fell, surely she'd be trampled.

Just when Julie thought she couldn't hang on another second, Hurricane came to a dead stop at the creek's edge. Julie didn't remember letting go. She didn't remember flying through the air. All she knew was the smack of cold water and the bite of a large rock under her shoulder. The wind was knocked out of her. She took in a ragged breath and scrambled backward on all fours like a crab to get away from Hurricane, who was calmly taking a drink.

"Julie, are you okay?" April asked, helping her to her feet. "Oh no, you're sopping wet. You look like a drowned rat!" She began to giggle.

"It's not funny," said Julie. "I almost got trampled. And after I fell, I could hardly even breathe."

April picked up the lead rope. "You'll be okay. Falling is part of learning to ride. You have to fall at least seven times before you're a good rider."

"Well, forget about learning to ride, then," Julie muttered. "I'm not getting back up on that horse."

"Oh, don't be such a baby. Look, I won't let go of the rope this time, and we'll just stay at a walk."

"I'm not a baby," said Julie, but her voice came out all wobbly and her legs felt like spaghetti. The girls headed back across the field in silence.

"Hey, Julie, just think—this is kind of like the time

in *Little House on the Prairie* when Nellie fell off Laura's horse," said April.

Julie glowered at her cousin. "For your information," she snapped, "that was just in the TV show. The *real* Laura never took Nellie riding—she took her into the stream so that Nellie would get leeches on her legs."

"Leeches? Eeww!" April began to giggle. But this time it didn't make Julie laugh.

June 20, after lunch

I don't care what April or anybody says. I'm not getting back on that horse—ever.

June 20, later

I re-read On the Banks of Plum Creek *for seven whole miles. Translation: I am not talking to April.*

Reading about pioneers is not the same as doing it. Riding Hurricane wasn't like what I imagined. Trying to stay on a bareback horse was harder than turning a cartwheel on the balance beam at gymnastics with Ivy. Maybe it wasn't so hard for Laura when she sat bareback on one of Pa's plow horses, but Hurricane is no plow horse, that's for sure.

Here's what's really bugging me: April thinks she knows all about horses and riding, but she should not have let go of the rope. I could have been hurt. Then she wouldn't have been laughing!

April and Tracy are taking a magazine quiz: are you more like a marshmallow or a carrot? What a dumb question.

I miss Ivy. And Mom. And Dad. And my nice private bedroom with no dumb giggling teenagers.

I never would have made it as a pioneer. Why did I even come on this trip?

At camp that night, Julie helped Uncle Buddy start the cook fire. As she crumpled newspaper for kindling, a picture of an old man holding up a flag caught her eye. "Oldest Man in State Raises Old Glory," the headline said.

"Look at this," she said to Uncle Buddy, showing him the article. "The oldest man in Pennsylvania is a hundred and one years old! His name is Mr. Witherspoon, and he lives in a town called Hershey. It says he hangs his flag out every day."

"A hundred and one? Wow, that's old, all right," said Uncle Buddy.

"Hershey—isn't that where they make Hershey's chocolate bars?" Tracy piped up.

"Yup," said Jimmy, "and we'll be going through Hershey next week. There's a big theme park, and we get to spend a whole day there."

"You'll love Hersheypark," April gushed. "It has great roller coasters, and a skyride, and everything!" Tracy looked excited, but Julie didn't say anything. She loved theme parks, too, but she still wasn't talking to April.

After supper, Tracy and April went into the tent to play a game Tracy had brought called Mystery Date. Julie heard gales of laughter coming out of the glowing tent. She sat alone on a log, poking a stick into the dying embers.

Aunt Catherine came over and sat down beside her. "You were awfully quiet today. Everything okay, honey?" Julie nodded. "You've had a long day. Don't you think you should get to bed?"

"I'm not sleepy," Julie replied. How could she read in the tent, with April and Tracy laughing their heads off?

"That was some fall you took today," Aunt Catherine said gently. "First time's always the worst."

Julie could not keep her lip from quivering. Aunt Catherine put an arm around her and the two sat in the comfort of the quiet dark.

"Have you ever heard the story of Lightning Kelley?" asked her aunt, breaking the silence.

"Who's that?" Julie asked.

"He was your great-great-great-grandfather Elijah Kelley, but everyone called him Lightning."

"Why?" asked Julie. "Was he famous?"

"Sure was, in his day. You've heard of the Pony Express, right? In 1860, that was the fastest way to get mail through the Wild West all the way to California."

"Yeah, we learned about it in school," said Julie, sitting up straighter. "But I never knew that I was related to one of the riders."

"Lightning was only seventeen when he joined up," said Aunt Catherine, "but he could ride a horse like nobody's business. They say he braved robbers, snowstorms, and mountain lions riding for the Pony Express. One time when he was crossing a river, the current was so strong that his horse got swept away right out from under him. He grabbed those saddle-bags full of mail, held them high over his head with the river raging all around, and saved the mail. Not a single letter was lost."

"Was his horse okay?" asked Julie.

"Yes, the story goes that he met up with his mustang three miles downriver." Aunt Catherine smiled. "Now, it really is time for bed."

Julie crawled into her sleeping bag, as soft and warm as flannel pajamas. Tracy and April were already asleep. Quietly, Julie flicked on her flashlight and opened her journal one more time.

June 20, nighttime

Lightning Kelley didn't let anything stop him. It's pretty cool to be related to him!

I wonder what he would have thought if he'd seen me flying off Hurricane and landing in the creek today.

Okay, he probably would have laughed. I suppose it did *look sort of funny. But I'm still not going to ride that horse again.*

The next morning, Julie slept late. When she emerged from the tent, Tracy was already back from the showers, trying to dry her long hair over the last of the coals from the morning campfire. "How's the shoulder?" she asked.

"Okay, I guess," Julie mumbled, rubbing it. Her shoulder was a little sore, but that wasn't what was bothering her. She took a bite of cold oatmeal.

"Are you still sulking because you fell off that horse?" Tracy asked.

"It's not just that." Julie wanted to tell her sister how let down she felt about the whole trip. She was scared to ride a horse. What was worse, being friends with April felt impossible. But most of all, she was disappointed in herself. She could feel the disappointment making a lump in her throat to go with the lump in her stomach. She pushed the cold oatmeal away.

"You know, Jules, April was just trying to do something nice for you. She knew how much you wanted to ride a horse."

Deep down, Julie knew Tracy was right. But the

disappointment wouldn't go away.

For the first hours of the morning, Julie decided to walk. It felt good to move, and the sun was warm on her face. She hiked alongside the docile workhorses. *If only Hurricane had been as quiet as Mack and Molly,* she thought wistfully.

In the afternoon, the wagon train began a long climb uphill. Each wagon went at its own pace. Their own wagon slowed to a snail's crawl, dropping behind the others. After several hours had gone by, Julie peered into the distance. The road dipped and curved around an outcropping of massive rock, but there wasn't another wagon in sight. She couldn't even spot the green station wagon with the flying flag that always followed the wagon train. And they hadn't passed a town all afternoon. There were just rocks, hills, and trees as far as the eye could see. The only sound was the constant buzz-saw humming of cicadas.

Was this how Laura Ingalls had felt crossing the long, lonely, empty prairie? Suddenly Julie missed the familiar honking horns and friendly cable-car bells of San Francisco.

As the shadows grew longer, the hill grew steeper, and Julie could hear Mack and Molly breathing hard as they strained into their collars. Their coats gleamed with sweat. She trudged beside the workhorses, feeling sorry for them.

April poked her head out the front of the wagon. "How much farther do we have to go today?" she asked her parents.

"Mr. Wescott said we have to make it to the top of this mountain by nightfall." Uncle Buddy looked over his shoulder at the setting sun. "I'm guessing it's only a few miles more, if we're lucky."

"But the sun's already going down," said April. "Where's Jimmy? I wish he'd ride back and tell us how much farther we have to go."

Without warning, the wagon lurched hard to the right and jerked to a stop. "Whooaa!" Uncle Buddy called to the horses. He set the brake and jumped down from the leaning wagon.

"Is everybody okay?" Aunt Catherine asked.

"We're okay," said Tracy. "But what happened?"

"Did we hit something?" asked April.

They scrambled down off the wagon. Aunt Catherine shone the flashlight while Uncle Buddy squatted on the ground to check under the right side of the wagon. Julie heard Uncle Buddy catch his breath as the flashlight played over the front wheel. It was stuck in a pothole and bent at an odd angle.

"Is the wheel broken?" April asked.

"I'm not sure," Uncle Buddy said tightly. He crouched lower, peering underneath the wagon. "The wheel seems all right—it's the axle I'm worried about. We'll have to get the wagon up out of this hole so I can take a better look."

"Maybe we could help push," Tracy suggested.

"You read my mind, Trace. Catherine, you drive," said Uncle Buddy. "The rest of us will push."

On the count of three, Aunt Catherine snapped the reins and called out, "Giddap! Come on, Mack. Come on, Molly. Let's go!"

"Push," Uncle Buddy ordered.

The horses strained, and the wagon rocked and creaked, but it wouldn't budge. Julie's sore shoulder smarted, and her arms ached from pushing so hard.

"Hold on while I take another look at that wheel," said Uncle Buddy.

Night had fallen. The humming cicadas had given way to a chorus of crickets and frogs, broken by the lonely hoot of an owl.

What if we're stranded here all night, and the wagon train leaves without us in the morning? Julie wondered. She stole a glance at her cousin. April was chewing a fingernail. *That's exactly what I do when I'm worried,* Julie thought as the last of her hurt and anger melted away.

Julie walked over and nudged her cousin. "This is kind of like in *Little House on the Prairie* when they were trying to cross a rushing river in their covered wagon," she said. "Pa had to jump into the cold water and swim out in front of the horses to pull them across. Remember?"

April nodded. "And Laura thought they were going to drown, but they made it."

"Girls," Aunt Catherine said, handing a box down to Tracy, "we have to empty this wagon."

"Unload *all* our stuff?" April asked.

"If we lighten the load, we just might get the wagon up out of this hole."

Box by box, one suitcase after another, they lowered everything out of the wagon. The luggage, tents, coolers, and gear made a heap by the roadside.

Clip-clop, clip-clop, clip-clop. A horse's hooves echoed over the night sounds.

"Did you hear that?" asked Tracy, shining her flashlight up and down the road. Like a ghost rider, Jimmy appeared in the small circle of light.

"Where have you guys been?" he asked. "They won't hold up the whole train for one wagon, you know. If you can't keep up, they'll leave without you in the morning."

"We're stuck!" said April. "It's not like we did it on purpose."

"Boy, are we glad to see you," said Tracy. "We need more hands to help push."

Uncle Buddy came over and handed Jimmy the end of a rope. "Maybe Hurricane can help pull us out of this hole. Here, let's run this rope from your saddle to the wagon. April, you lead Hurricane so that Jimmy can help us push."

"How far is camp?" Aunt Catherine asked.

"Twenty minutes ahead, once you crest that hill,"

said Jimmy, looping a half hitch around his saddle horn.
He dismounted and handed Hurricane's reins to April.

"Okay, let's try it again," said Uncle Buddy after
he'd tied the rope to the wagon. "One, two, three,
push!"

Hurricane and the workhorses strained forward.
Julie, Tracy, Jimmy, and Uncle Buddy leaned against
the back of the wagon and heaved. The wagon gave one
loud groan, then lurched over the rim of the pothole.

"Hooray!" the girls cheered.

"C'mon," said Tracy. "The sooner we load back up,
the sooner we get to camp. I'm starving."

Aunt Catherine surveyed the pile. "Girls, this is
just too much for the horses to haul up this mountain.
We're going to have to make some tough choices and
leave some of our things behind."

The cousins looked at one another, stunned. "Mom,
we can't just—" April began to protest, but Aunt Catherine was already separating some of the pots and pans.

Tracy opened both of her suitcases and began divid-
ing her things. Into the smaller suitcase went her Mystery Date board game, bathrobe, hair dryer, and extra
sweatshirt. She picked up her pioneer dress.

"Not your dress!" said Julie. "You'll want to wear it to the big barn dance when we get to Valley Forge."

"No I won't," said Tracy, stuffing it into the suitcase with her other castoffs. "I look like a dork in that thing."

Julie wasn't about to leave *her* dress behind. But then she thought of Mack and Molly sweating and straining to pull the heavy wagon up the mountain. She thought of Laura Ingalls and the time her family moved to Kansas and had to leave even their beds and chairs and tables behind.

Pulling her suitcase from the pile, Julie lifted out her set of *Little House* books. If the soldiers at Valley Forge could go a whole winter without shoes and coats, she could do without her books. She took one last look at them and then set the books on the leave-behind pile at the side of the road.

April gasped. "Mom, don't make Julie give up her books. I'll leave my board games and my magazines and—"

"It's okay," Julie told her cousin. "I know all the stories by heart."

"But what will you do now when you're mad at

me?" April asked, putting her arm around Julie.

June 21

We (finally!) made it to camp. April and I shouted as soon as we saw the wagons. April always says they look like giant loaves of Wonder Bread. She cracks me up!

Tonight the wagons were circled together around the flickering campfire. It felt like coming home.

Making History

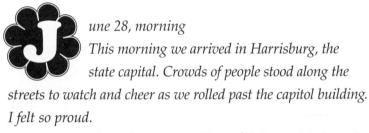

une 28, morning
This morning we arrived in Harrisburg, the
state capital. Crowds of people stood along the
streets to watch and cheer as we rolled past the capitol building.
I felt so proud.

We stopped at a large post office to pick up a big box of
scrolls. There was a line of people still signing them as we
arrived. A girl my age handed me a bunch of scrolls. She
said her Girl Scout troop had been gathering signatures
since Easter.

Afterward, I mailed postcards to Mom, Dad, and Ivy.

June 28, after lunch

April keeps bugging me to ride Hurricane again. She
says whenever you fall off a horse, you have to get right back

on. I got up my nerve to feed him an apple this morning, but
no way am I getting on his back again.

❀

By the time the wagon train pulled into Hershey
that night, Julie and Tracy had been on the road for two
weeks, April's family had been traveling even longer,
and everyone was looking forward to a day off.

The next morning after breakfast, April bubbled with
excitement about the theme park. Julie couldn't wait to
go on the rides, but something was nagging at her.

"Why do I feel like I know something important
about Hershey?" she asked.

"Maybe because it's famous for Hershey bars?"
Tracy said drily.

"And Hershey's chocolate kisses—yum!" April
added.

"No, it's something else," Julie said, frowning. Then
she remembered—the night after she fell off Hurricane,
when she'd helped Uncle Buddy make a fire. The oldest
man in Pennsylvania lived in Hershey!

"Hey, April, what if we got Mr. Witherspoon to sign
one of the scrolls? He's the oldest man in Pennsylvania—

a hundred and one years old—and he lives right here in Hershey!"

"Let's go ask Mr. Sweeney," said April. The girls scurried around the wagons, looking for Mr. Sweeney. They found him sitting on the back of his wagon eating a sandwich. He greeted the girls with his usual cheerful smile. Julie asked him about Mr. Witherspoon.

"Ooh, yes, I read that newspaper story," said Mr. Sweeney. "Wouldn't it be something to get his signature on one of our scrolls? But girls, I don't see how it's humanly possible. He lives ten miles out of town, and there isn't time to arrange to send somebody out there. Mr. Wescott has given the outriders the day off." He shrugged good-naturedly and took another bite of his sandwich. "Too bad, though. Michigan Bob would be green with envy!"

"Who's Michigan Bob?" Julie asked.

"An old pal of mine who's collecting scrolls on the Great Lakes route. I hear he's been bragging since Detroit about some World Series pitcher who signed one of his scrolls. He's hoping to be chosen to present the scroll for President Ford to sign. The Bicentennial committee hasn't yet decided who gets to do the honors,

but that signature might put me in the running!"
He winked at the girls and gulped a drink from his
canteen.

"Oh well, it was a good idea, anyway," said April
as they strolled back to their wagon. "Hey, look, there
it is—Hersheypark!" In the distance, the highest tracks
of a roller coaster arched above the trees. "C'mon, let's
hurry. Don't you just love roller coasters?"

Julie did love them, but somehow riding a roller
coaster didn't seem as exciting—or as important—as
getting Mr. Witherspoon's signature. In the back of her
mind, an idea was forming. It seemed impossible, but it
wouldn't go away.

"April, listen. Mr. Sweeney said it's not *humanly*
possible, but what about a horse?"

"Julie, what are you talking about?" April asked
without breaking her stride.

"We could ride Hurricane out to where Mr. Witherspoon lives. That way we could get his signature."

April stopped in her tracks. "What about Hersheypark?"

"I guess we'd miss it," Julie admitted. "But you
can go another time, and we have theme parks in

California, too. Come on, April—I can't do it by myself. Do you think Jimmy would let us borrow Hurricane? Would your parents let us go?"

April considered. "Well, I don't see why not. I can handle Hurricane like he's Lassie. I could ride in front, and you could ride double behind me, and we'd be together the whole time. But do you really want to? I thought you were afraid to get back on him."

Julie gave a weak smile. Her stomach did a somersault just thinking about her last ride and how close she had come to being trampled. Could she really muster the courage to climb back on that horse? She remembered the story Mom had once told her about her own horse, Firefly, and how she got spooked and acted crazy the time she was stung by a bee. What if Hurricane got stung, or spooked by a snake? Julie's legs turned to liquid.

But she didn't let on to April. Lightning Kelley hadn't let a raging river stop him from delivering the mail. And weren't she and April both related to him? "C'mon," Julie urged, tugging on her cousin's sleeve. "Let's go—before I lose my nerve."

While Julie studied a map, April saddled up and mounted Hurricane. "Just put your foot in the stirrup and grab the saddle horn. It's easy." Julie swung up onto Hurricane's rump behind the saddle and held tight to April's waist.

"How did the pioneers ever ride horses in long dresses?" Julie wondered aloud, grateful for her blue jeans.

One nudge from April and they were off. Hurricane started out at a walk. Julie tried to relax and settle in to the rhythm.

"You okay back there?" asked April.

"I think so," Julie said nervously, trying to steady her voice. "It's kind of slippery."

"We'll take it easy, don't worry."

As they rode along, Julie felt more confident and began to enjoy the ride. But her spirits dropped when they reached the first intersection and she checked the map. "We've been riding at least half an hour and we've only gone two miles. We have eight more miles to go. We'll never make it!"

April hesitated. "Do you want to turn back?"

"No, but . . . what can we do?" Julie's stomach tightened. She knew the answer.

April urged Hurricane across the intersection and onto the grassy shoulder beside the road. "Let's try a nice smooth canter. You can do it. Ready?"

"Okay," said Julie in a small, shaky voice.

As soon as Hurricane took off, Julie started bouncing and sliding. "Stop!" she shouted. "I can't hold on. I'm slipping off!"

"Whoa," said April, pulling on the reins. When Hurricane came to a stop, Julie clung to April, her heart pounding.

"I have an idea," said April. "You should ride in front so that you can hold on to the saddle horn and put your feet in the stirrups. That'll make it easier for you."

"But I don't know how to steer or work the reins."

"I'll show you," said April. "It's easy."

"Stop saying it's easy!" said Julie. "It's not easy for me."

"Sorry," April said. She dismounted and helped Julie slide forward into the saddle. Then she climbed

back on behind Julie and showed her how to hold
the reins and guide the horse. "When you're ready to
canter, lean forward a little and squeeze his sides with
your heels, gently."

Swallowing her fear, Julie did as April had instructed. Hurricane sprang forward, but since Julie was
already leaning forward, she kept her balance.

"Good!" April exclaimed. "That's it!"

"It feels . . . almost like a rocking horse, once you get
used to it," said Julie. She was still gripping the horn
tightly, but she no longer felt as if she were going to fall.
"I think I'm getting the hang of it."

"You're doing great! I knew you could do it. You're
a natural."

"I'm riding," said Julie. "I'm riding Hurricane!"

As the girls dismounted, a green station wagon
flying an American flag pulled away from the curb
in front of Mr. Witherspoon's house.

"Hey, that was the souvenir guy," April said.
"I wonder what he's doing here."

Despite the warm summer day, Mr. Witherspoon

sat on a front porch glider with a blanket over his lap. His pale blue eyes smiled at Julie from a deeply lined face. "Is the Pony Express delivering my mail today?" he asked. He chuckled at his own joke, but his laugh turned into a cough.

Julie pulled Hurricane to a halt next to the man's porch. "I'm Julie and this is my cousin April. We're from the Bicentennial wagon train. But our great-great-great-grandfather really *did* ride for the Pony Express. His name was Elijah Kelley, but everyone called him Lightning Kelley."

Mr. Witherspoon squinted at them. "Lightning Kelley, eh?"

"We brought a scroll for you to sign," said April, taking it out of the saddlebag.

"It's a special scroll for the Bicentennial," Julie explained, suddenly worried. What if he didn't want to sign it? "If you sign the scroll, it means that you dedicate yourself to the ideas in the Declaration of Independence." There, that sounded impressive.

Mr. Witherspoon frowned. "You're not planning to sell this now, are you? 'Cause the fella who was just here wanted to sell my autograph for money. Even offered *me* money for it. Imagine that." The old man shook his head. "Guess he doesn't know my family's history isn't for sale."

"We'd never sell it," said Julie. "The scroll will be in a museum at Valley Forge." She offered him the clipboard with the scroll.

Mr. Witherspoon reached out a shaky hand and took it. Adjusting his glasses, he squinted at the heading. Then he looked back up at Julie and April. "You girls know about the Declaration of Independence?" Julie and April nodded. "Well here's something I bet you didn't know. *My* great-great-great-great-grandfather didn't ride for the Pony Express—but he *did* sign the Declaration of Independence."

Julie looked at April and then back at Mr. Witherspoon, her eyes round with amazement. "For real?"

Mr. Witherspoon nodded, his blue eyes crinkling into a smile. "Say, how would you girls like to see a rare copy of the Declaration that's been in my family for a hundred and fifty years?"

"We'd love to," Julie breathed.

With effort, Mr. Witherspoon got up from his porch swing. He went inside and returned carrying a slender leather tube. "My hands don't work so well anymore," he said, handing the tube to Julie.

Carefully, Julie and April opened it and slid out a delicate, tea-colored parchment. As they slowly unrolled it, Julie's eyes fell on the sacred words: *We hold these truths to be self-evident, that all men are created equal . . .*

"And there's John Hancock," said April, pointing at the first signature, with its swirling, looping flourish.

The old man pointed a crooked finger at his ancestor's name in the large cluster of signatures at the bottom. Julie leaned in closer. It was a little hard to read, but she could make it out—John Witherspoon. "Wow, he was really there in 1776. Just think—that means he knew Benjamin Franklin and Thomas Jefferson!" Julie looked up, her eyes shining. "You sure are lucky to have this."

"It was lost for many, many years," said Mr. Witherspoon. "Then one day my mother was getting an old painting framed, and there it was, hidden behind the picture."

"Thank you for showing us," said April, carefully helping Julie roll it back up and slide it into the tube.

"Now, where's that scroll of yours?" the old man

asked. "Time for me to sign *my* John Hancock. Or should I say John Witherspoon? All I need is my quill pen." He reached into his pocket.

"You have a quill pen?" Julie asked, wide-eyed.

His eyes twinkling, Mr. Witherspoon took out an ordinary ballpoint pen, working himself into another fit of laughter. He started to write, but nothing came out. "Fiddlesticks!" he said, flipping the paper over and scribbling on the back until ink came out.

"Hey, that scribble looks kind of like the loops under John Hancock's name," April remarked.

Mr. Witherspoon turned the scroll back over and signed his name on the first line.

Standing on the porch, Julie gazed at his signature on the scroll and then at the tube that held the copy of the Declaration. She felt as if somehow a line had been drawn, a line from some long-ago, dusty past that connected her, today, in 1976, with the birth of the nation two hundred years ago.

June 29 (already?!)

Tracy told me I was crazy to miss Hersheypark. She said it has the best roller coaster ever and lots of FREE chocolate, too!

But riding Hurricane was way more exciting than any roller coaster. Coming home, we rode as fast as Lightning! (Get it?) And when April and I handed that scroll to Mr. Sweeney and told him how Mr. Witherspoon's great-great-great-great-grandfather had been one of the signers of the Declaration, he could hardly believe it. "Wait till Michigan Bob hears about this!" he said. "That'll put a stop to his bragging."

I think this was one of the best days of my life.

Valley Forge

uly 3, morning
We made it to Valley Forge!

All around us, the grassy, rolling hills look as pretty as a postcard. There's a tiny town, but most of Valley Forge is a park, with rows and rows of cannons. I wonder if they're all the way from the time of George Washington.

Huge crowds are here for the Bicentennial—Mr. Wescott says tens of thousands of people, plus hundreds of wagons. Just think of all the journeys people have taken to get here. I bet everyone has a story to tell!

Today there's a parade of all the wagons, and tonight is the barn dance. And then tomorrow is July 4, and the president will be here! I hope Dad makes it in time to see him.

Still, even with all the excitement, I'm a little sad, too, because it's the end of our trip.

That evening, after a potluck supper with several other families from their wagon train, the three girls huddled inside the wagon getting ready for the barn dance.

Julie squirmed into her pioneer dress. "Do you think I should put my hair in braids, like Laura?" she asked April.

"I'd leave it loose," said April. She had on a pioneer dress, too. "Are you going to wear your bonnet?"

"Of course! Gosh, pioneers sure had to do a lot of buttons," Julie remarked.

"That's because nobody had invented the zipper yet," said Tracy, zipping up her jeans.

"Tracy, aren't you going to the dance?" April asked.

"Yeah—I'm already dressed," Tracy said, coming over to help. She fastened the top buttons on Julie's dress and tied a big bow in the sash of April's apron. "You two look so pretty," she added a bit wistfully, turning the girls around to face her.

"Too bad you left your pioneer dress behind," said Julie.

"I know," Tracy admitted. "Everybody'll be in costume tonight. I'm going to stick out like a sore thumb."

"Knock, knock," called Jimmy from outside the wagon.

"No boys allowed," said April as Tracy opened the back flap.

Jimmy looked up at Tracy, holding one hand behind his back and grinning. He was wearing a fringed buckskin jacket. His boots were shined and his hair was combed. Julie thought he looked very handsome.

"Somebody's not going to be filling up her dance card tonight," he said to Tracy, pointing at her blue jeans.

"Are *you* going to give me grief, too?" Tracy groaned, but Julie could tell she was kidding.

Jimmy gave her a taunting look. "What would you give to be able to wear that dress you left behind to the barn dance tonight?"

"Oh, let me think," said Tracy. "How 'bout a million dollars?"

"Then you owe me a million dollars," said Jimmy, calling her bluff. He held out a small bundle of cloth tied with twine. "Pay up!"

"My pioneer dress! I don't get it—how did you—?" Tracy sputtered, but Julie could tell she was pleased.

"I rescued it that night you guys got stuck up on the mountain," Jimmy told her.

"I can't believe it! Where have you been hiding it all this time—Hurricane's saddlebags?"

"Nope, my mom hid it."

"Aunt Catherine, you were in on this, too?" Tracy called.

"Guilty as charged," Aunt Catherine called back. "Now hurry and get dressed. We don't want to be late!"

"That was *so* much fun!" Julie gasped as she and April collapsed on a bale of straw. They had just learned how to square dance. It was a hot night, and the girls had worked up a sweat swinging each other to the lively fiddle music.

"I know—let's cool off by ducking for apples again!" said April. But before they could head to the game area, Aunt Catherine cornered them.

"Time to go, buffalo gals. We've got another big day tomorrow."

"Boy, could I ever use a shower," Tracy said as the cousins walked back to their campsite. "Good thing I don't have to wear this dress again!" She twirled around, making her skirt bell out, and then linked elbows with April and spun her around. Uncle Buddy plucked a few notes on his banjo, while Julie clapped in rhythm, calling, "Swing your partner round and round!"

Suddenly, out of nowhere, Mr. Sweeney came rushing up behind them. "Julie, April—the scroll," he gasped. "It's gone."

July 3, I mean 4

We searched until after midnight, and we still can't find the scroll with Mr. Witherspoon's signature. At first, I was sure it had to be somewhere in Mr. Sweeney's wagon. But it's not, and Mr. Sweeney is convinced it was stolen!

Tracy tried to cheer me up by reminding me that there are still more than twenty million signatures to present to the president. That's a lot of signatures. But are any of them from somebody whose ancestor signed the Declaration of Independence?

The next morning, Julie smelled bacon frying. *Why didn't Mom wake me up for breakfast?* she wondered sleepily. Blinking one eye open, she realized she wasn't in her bed back in San Francisco. *Pop, pop, POP!* Firecrackers...it was the Fourth of July...she was in Valley Forge, Pennsylvania, on the day of the biggest birthday celebration the country had ever seen. And Dad would be coming today! Julie felt over-the-moon happy. Jump-out-of-bed excited. Then, halfway out of her sleeping bag, she remembered—the missing scroll.

The whole campground seemed to crackle with excitement. Maybe they'd found the scroll while she was sleeping! But as soon as she saw Mr. Sweeney's face, she knew.

"We've searched everywhere," Mr. Sweeney was telling her aunt and uncle. "I have a suspicion, though. That Clark Higgins, the one who's been selling souvenirs out of his station wagon—we heard he was after that signature."

April spoke up. "Julie and I saw him that day at Mr. Witherspoon's!"

"It's wrong to sell Mr. Witherspoon's signature for money," said Julie. "I promised him it wouldn't be sold. Can't we make the souvenir guy give it back?"

Mr. Sweeney shook his head. "We would if we could find him. But Mr. Wescott ran him off again yesterday for selling without a permit."

After breakfast, Julie and April braided ribbons and wildflowers into Hurricane's mane so that he would look his best for the presentation of the scrolls to President Ford. The color guard started the ceremony with a flag raising and the Pledge of Allegiance. Everyone sang the national anthem, and then the governor of Pennsylvania took the podium to read the Declaration of Independence.

"I can't see," said Julie, standing on tiptoe and craning her neck.

"Here, sit up on Hurricane," said Jimmy. He dismounted and handed her the reins.

"You mean it?" Julie put one foot in the stirrup, heaved herself up, and settled into the saddle. It was hard to believe that only a week ago, she'd been afraid of Hurricane.

"Make way," said April, climbing up to sit behind Julie. "Wow, what a view!"

Before them were hundreds of covered wagons that looked like ships in an ocean of people. The fifty official state wagons were fanned out in formation, flags flying.

"Here, these'll make the view even better," said Jimmy, handing April his field glasses. April took a turn and then passed them to Julie.

Julie scanned the colorful crowds. People of all ages were wearing everything from tie-dyed sundresses to cowboy chaps to Revolutionary War uniforms. Flags of all sizes flapped in the breeze.

Wait a minute. Julie trained the binoculars on a stand of trees across the field and fiddled with the focus knob. Through the leaves, she thought she saw a familiar-looking flag—familiar because it was attached to the antenna of a green station wagon.

"I'll be right back." Before April could ask questions, Julie slipped down off Hurricane and began weaving her way through the crowds. She ran as best she could, dodging horses, strollers, kids, dogs, and

Frisbees. At last she reached the station wagon, half-hidden in a grove of trees.

"Hey!" Julie waved her arms. "Aren't you Mr. Higgins?"

A skinny man with a mustache turned and gave her a friendly smile. "That's me. I got hats, flags, T-shirts, cuff links, you name it. I'm your official Bicentennial souvenir shop."

"No you're not," said Julie. "You're not even allowed to be here. I'm reporting you to the wagon master."

"Now hold on just a Ben Franklin minute!" said Mr. Higgins. "What'd I do?"

"Where is it?" Julie demanded. "The scroll with Mr. Witherspoon's signature—the one you stole."

Mr. Higgins's head snapped back and his eyes opened wide. Julie had to admit he looked genuinely surprised. "For your information, missy, I got a seller's permit to be here today." He pulled an official-looking paper with a Bicentennial seal from his pocket. "Go ahead—search my car if you like. I got nothing to hide."

Julie poked her head into the back of the station wagon, but all she could see were boxes and trays of cheap souvenirs. "Well," she stammered, "then how come you're hiding under these trees?"

"A little thing called shade," said Mr. Higgins, pointing to the leafy branches overhead. "It's gonna be a scorcher today."

Julie didn't want to believe him, but she knew she couldn't prove he had stolen the scroll. She didn't feel that she had the right to search his car. Besides, if he had stolen the scroll because it was valuable, he probably had it safely stashed in a hotel room somewhere.

The president was going to arrive at any moment, and Julie didn't want to miss seeing him. She broke into a run, trying to dodge through the line of official state wagons, but a crowd of people blocked her path. In front of them, newspaper photographers were taking pictures of a man standing at the front of one of the wagons.

"Michigan Bob, what are you going to say to the president?" a reporter called.

Julie paused. "What's going on?" she asked a young woman standing nearby.

"Didn't you hear? Michigan Bob is going to present the scrolls to the president. He has a scroll with a famous signature—"

"Oh, right, a baseball pitcher," said Julie with a nod, remembering what Mr. Sweeney had told her.

"No, this one's from some guy whose ancestor signed the Declaration of Independence," said the woman. "At least, that's what I heard."

Julie drew in a sharp breath. True, there could be many descendants of the original signers, but it was such a coincidence . . . *Something's funny about this,* she thought, frowning. She stepped away from the crowd to get a better look at the wagon. On the side of the wagon, MICHIGAN was painted in big blue letters above a picture of the Great Lakes.

There was no time to waste. Julie darted to the far end of the wagon and quickly climbed into the back. Desperately she looked around. She knew she was trespassing, but what if the missing scroll was here? It was a slim chance, just a hunch, but she had to take it. Her heart thumped wildly.

She spotted a makeshift desk covered with a jumble of papers. There they were—a whole stack of scrolls! *There must be hundreds here,* she thought. *How will I ever find it?* She picked up a pile of scrolls and began leafing through them.

"Hey—you there! What do you think you're doing?"

Startled, Julie dropped the stack of papers in her hands. "I'm sorry, I—" She bent down to gather up the mess.

"Don't touch those. Just get out." Michigan Bob had come in from the front of the wagon and was making his way toward her.

Julie stood frozen, her eyes riveted on a blank page. It was the back side of a scroll, blank except for a small squiggle of hand-drawn loops like the ones under the name John Hancock.

Julie snatched up the scroll and flipped it over. There, on the first line, was the name—*John Wither-spoon.*

"Hey, gimme that," said Michigan Bob, lunging for her. But Julie was already scrambling out of the wagon. "Come back here, you!" he shouted as Julie dashed past the crowd and zigzagged across the grassy field around people and dogs, wagons and folding chairs, heading for the Pennsylvania wagon train.

Clutching the scroll close to her chest, she ran like the wind. *Like lightning,* she couldn't help thinking. *Lightning Kelley.*

Julie was breathless by the time she reached Mr. Sweeney's wagon. Holding her ribs to ease the stabbing pain in her side, she waved the scroll at him, blurting out the whole story.

"You mean to tell me that Michigan Bob stole it right out from under my nose just so he could have his fifteen minutes of fame?" said Mr. Sweeney. "Well, I'll be a star-spangled banana! And to think I considered him a friend."

Word spread like wildfire through the Pennsylvania wagon train that the missing scroll had been found. Cheering and clapping erupted as more and more people heard the good news.

Julie's relatives crowded around, hugging her and patting her on the back. Suddenly Julie felt herself wrapped in a strong pair of arms and swung into the air. "How's my girl? I hear you're a hero!"

"Dad!" Julie squealed. "You made it! I missed you so much."

Dad's long hug told her he'd missed her, too.

"And I thought you just wanted to see better," said April, starting to giggle. "I didn't know you were going to go all Nancy Drew on us!" Everybody laughed.

The wagon master came over to shake hands with Julie. "I never would have figured it out," said Mr. Wescott. "But I'm awfully glad you did."

"Will Mr. Sweeney get to present the scroll for the president to sign?" Julie asked.

"It's all taken care of," said the wagon master.

"Time out—slight change of plans," Mr. Sweeney announced. "It was Julie who saved the day." He turned to Julie, handing her the scroll. "I think it's only right that you do the honors—present the scroll for President Ford to sign, and shake his hand."

Julie turned a glowing face to Dad. "Did you hear that? I'm going to shake hands with the president!"

Detention

hen she stopped to think about it, Julie couldn't decide which was the proudest moment of her life so far: saving the bald eagles, or shaking hands with the President of the United States. Her excitement lasted the rest of the summer and on into her first few days of fifth grade, as she retold the story of the wagon journey to Mom, Ivy, T. J., and her friends at Jack London Elementary.

But by the time school was in full swing, Julie's glow of excitement and pride had faded. One day in September, as she sat in class listening to the teacher lecture about early American explorers, she tried to distract herself by daydreaming about her summer—and realized that she could no longer recapture that wonderful feeling she'd had at the end of the wagon trip: the confidence that she could do something important, something that mattered, something that made a difference.

Maybe it was because her new teacher, Mrs. Duncan, was super-strict. She always wore buttoned-up blouses that pinched her neck. Even her hair was strict—starched and stiff as a ruler. She had warned the class about passing notes. "This is fifth grade, people," she'd been saying for the first few weeks of school.

So when a note landed on her desk in the middle of social studies class, Julie was intrigued, but cautious. Luckily Mrs. Duncan had her back turned as she wrote lessons on the board. Julie snatched the note and hid it in the opening of her desk. Her eyes darted around the room, making sure nobody had seen the special delivery.

As Mrs. Duncan explained about Lewis and Clark's trip through grizzly bear country toward the Rocky Mountains, Julie snuck a peek at the note. It was from Joy Jenner, who sat across the aisle from her.

The week before school started, Julie had noticed a new girl walking some of the neighborhood dogs—a Chihuahua, a toy poodle, and a cute, hairy mutt—at the park. Then, on the first day of fifth grade, there she was, in the same class! When Mrs. Duncan seated the class alphabetically by *first* name, Julie and Joy ended up next to each other.

A year ago, in fourth grade, Julie had been the new girl herself at Jack London Elementary, so she knew just how Joy felt. She was determined to help make Joy feel comfortable.

Julie glanced over at her new friend. Joy stopped fiddling with a strand of her reddish-brown hair. She leaned forward, her dark eyes intent on the teacher's face. Because Joy was deaf, she was trying to read Mrs. Duncan's lips, but she sometimes had difficulty understanding certain words. Julie knew Joy didn't like to ask questions in class—when she did, somebody always snickered at the funny-sounding way she talked.

Quietly, Julie opened the note. It said: *"A sack of wheat saved them?"*

Julie covered her mouth to stifle a giggle. She crossed out "sack of wheat" and wrote, *"Sac-a-ja-we-a, Lewis and Clark's Shoshone Indian guide."*

Julie tossed the note back to Joy just as Mrs. Duncan turned.

"Julie Albright, what have I said about passing notes?"

"Not to?" Julie asked.

"You and Miss Jenner have earned yourselves another demerit."

"But Mrs. Duncan, it's not what you think. Joy didn't understand—"

"No excuses." Mrs. Duncan pointed to the metal wastebasket. All eyes were on Julie as she trudged to the front of the room.

"Mrs. Duncan? The note's about our lesson," Julie said. "Honest. You can read it yourself."

"I don't want to argue. That's not how we do things in Room 5D."

Julie tried to explain further. "Joy was having some trouble reading your lips."

Joy stood and pointed to herself. In her halting, too-loud tone, she stammered, "It was my fault. Not Julie's. I passed the note."

"That's enough, both of you," Mrs. Duncan snapped. "I will not take up any more class time with this nonsense. This isn't the first time I've had to speak to you about this. You will both report to detention after school. Three o'clock sharp."

Joy looked as if she'd been stung.

"But we only have two demerits," Julie protested.

"Unless you want a whole *week* of detention, you will sit down immediately. Both of you." Mrs. Duncan set her lips in a thin, straight line.

Joy slumped down into the hard wooden desk chair. Julie's face flushed red and she fumed all the way back to her seat. Snickers spread through the class.

"Any of you are welcome to join them in detention," Mrs. Duncan added sharply. "Now take out your silent reading. I want fifteen minutes of quiet."

Fifth grade was no fair.

I will not pass notes in class.
I will not pass notes in class.
I will not pass notes in class.

Julie could not imagine writing the same sentence over and over one hundred times. Her hand hurt just thinking about it. Then she had to write *I will not talk back to the teacher* one hundred times. That sentence was even longer!

Joy sat hunched over her paper, biting her bottom

lip. Julie and Joy were the only two girls at the detention table, along with several boys, including a sixth grader everybody called Stinger.

Stinger had reddish blond hair that fell over his eyes. Julie had heard the stories about him. Stinger was always picking fights on the playground and stealing kids' lunch money or tossing their bag lunches into the toilet in the boys' bathroom.

Julie rotated her wrist in circles. Her hand felt as if it were falling off and she was only on sentence number forty-nine. She picked up a magazine and leafed through it.

"Hey, no reading magazines in detention," Stinger called out, pointing.

All heads turned. Stinger got up and ambled over to Julie and Joy.

"Mr. Stenger, back to your seat. You'll recall there's also a *No talking* rule in detention," said Mr. Arnold, the vice principal. His brown mustache bristled up like a fuzzy caterpillar. "Miss Albright? Are you finished with your sentences?"

"No . . . I think I have writer's cramp. I was just giving my hand a rest for a second," Julie explained, hoping she wasn't in even more trouble.

"Back to work, everyone," said Mr. Arnold, glancing at the clock. "We still have half an hour to go."

Julie heaved a sigh and returned to her paper. She was missing shooting hoops with T. J. for this? What a waste.

Finishing her first one hundred sentences, Julie started on the next. Joy looked up and caught her eye. Julie pointed to her paper and then twirled her finger near her temple. She wondered if the sign for "cuckoo" was the same in sign language.

Joy grinned and giggled, copying Julie's "cuckoo" motion.

"Mr. Arnold, they're talking," Stinger said.

"I didn't hear anything," said Mr. Arnold, looking up over his reading glasses.

"That's 'cause they're talking with their hands. I swear."

Mr. Arnold came over to the detention table. "Mr. Stenger, it looks to me like the girls are well ahead of you. Do you need to come up and sit next to me?"

"No, sir," said Stinger.

Julie turned back to her paper. One hour of detention

felt like a week. She glanced at a poster near the window. It had a photo of a kitten clinging to a thin branch with the words *Hang in there, baby!*

Only seventy-four more lines to go.

The minute detention let out, Julie was bursting to talk. Joy had to ask Julie to slow down.

"Sorry," said Julie, turning to look directly at Joy so that Joy could read her lips. "It's just that detention is such a waste!"

"I know," Joy said. "I don't see what we learned from writing the same sentence for an hour."

"We learned about writer's cramp," said Julie. Joy laughed and made a gesture as if her hand were falling off. Julie laughed, too.

A stern voice behind them said, "Detention is no laughing matter." Julie spun around and there stood Stinger, elbowing his buddies. "Gotcha. I got you so good."

Joy motioned to Julie, pointing down the street. *Let's get out of here.*

"See you tomorrow," said Stinger. "At Detention Club."

"We're not going to be in detention again tomorrow," said Julie.

"Wanna bet? Duncan Donut passes out detentions like sprinkles on donuts. She gave me forty-three detentions last year. I hold the school record," he said proudly. "Till you girls came along."

"What was that about?" Joy asked Julie as they hurried down the sidewalk.

"He thinks we're his new detention buddies," said Julie, turning to face her friend. "But I hope we never have to go back there again. Ever."

Joy held out her thumb and little finger and motioned back and forth. Julie knew this sign meant *Me, too.* The girls turned the corner and headed up the hill toward their neighborhood.

"Why can't they just let us do homework in detention?" Joy asked.

"I guess that's not a punishment," said Julie. "But I don't see why we couldn't do something useful, like wash chalkboards or pick up litter on the playground."

"You should be principal," said Joy, circling the letter *P* over her left hand as she said the word *principal*. Julie grinned and nodded, pleased to learn a new sign. In the few weeks since school had started, Joy had taught her quite a few signs. The signs were interesting and fun to learn, like a secret code.

When the girls came to Belvedere Street, the two went separate ways, waving good-bye. Joy signed *See you later, alligator.* Julie paused, trying to remember what Joy had shown her, then signed, *After 'while, crocodile.* Joy covered her mouth, her eyes sparkling with laughter. She called, "You just said *After 'while, hippopotamus!*"

As soon as Julie got home, she ran upstairs, turned on the toaster oven, and fixed herself a plate of nachos dripping with cheese. Tracy walked in and grabbed a handful.

"Hey, get your own!" said Julie.

"Shooting hoops made you hungry, huh?" Tracy asked, wiping a hand on her jeans.

Julie snorted. "No, *detention* made me hungry."

"Oh, I forgot—you're a big bad fifth grader now."

Julie made a face and scooped up another cheesy chip. "Hey, Tracy, in high school, do they make you sit and write dumb old sentences for an hour in detention?"

"How would I know?" said Tracy. "I'm not one of the *bad* kids."

"No, seriously. What do they do in high school detention?"

"Well, I think they just let you sit there and you have to be quiet. You can't talk or chew gum or eat snacks or anything, but I think you're allowed to read or do your homework, stuff like that."

"No fair," said Julie, flicking on the TV and plopping down on the sofa. Tracy squeezed in next to her.

"You're not getting any more nachos," Julie warned, pulling the plate onto her lap.

"So, you're watching *Little House on the Prairie?* I thought you only liked the books," Tracy taunted.

Julie moved her hand away from her face, in the direction of her sister.

"What's that supposed to mean?" Tracy asked.

"It means *bug off!*" said Julie, laughing. "It's sign language. I learned it from Joy the other day. Besides, *Little House on the Prairie* reminds me of cousin April and our big trip last summer." Julie smiled at the memory.

"I know some sign language," said Tracy.

"Really?" Julie asked, turning toward her sister with interest.

Tracy mimed putting her fingertips to her mouth. "This is the sign for *more nachos.*"

Julie mimed back at her sister. "That's the sign for *ha ha, very funny.* Now, shush. Laura and Mary are coming on."

"But why isn't there any sound?" Tracy asked.

"I want to see what it would be like to have to read lips."

Poster Power

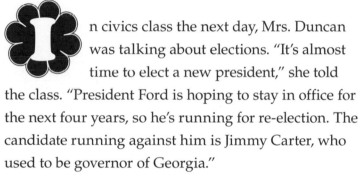I n civics class the next day, Mrs. Duncan was talking about elections. "It's almost time to elect a new president," she told the class. "President Ford is hoping to stay in office for the next four years, so he's running for re-election. The candidate running against him is Jimmy Carter, who used to be governor of Georgia."

"My dad's voting for Carter," said Beth.

"My dad says he's a peanut farmer!" interrupted David. "He wears sweaters like Mr. Rogers and smiles like a camel." The whole class burst out laughing.

"Interesting information, David," said Mrs. Duncan, two frown lines appearing on her brow.

Julie glanced across at Joy to see if she understood the conversation. They didn't dare pass notes in Mrs. Detention's class anymore.

"Class," said Mrs. Duncan, "your homework assignment is to read one newspaper article about Gerald Ford and one about Jimmy Carter."

Julie raised her hand. "Are we going to vote, like in an election?"

"Yes, as a matter of fact," said Mrs. Duncan. "But not for Ford or Carter," she added, flashing a rare smile. "We have school elections coming up for student body president. There will be an all-school assembly to get to know the candidates, and you'll each get to vote."

That afternoon, as Julie, Joy, and T. J. walked down the hall to their art class, Joy pointed to a new poster on the wall. It said,

> *You have a STEAK in Student Government!*
> *VOTE Salisbury for President.*

"Whoa, that's Mark Salisbury," said T. J.

"Who's he?" asked Joy.

"Only the most popular kid in sixth grade and probably the whole school," T. J. replied.

Julie frowned. "Have a *steak* in government? Give me a break. It's spelled S-T-A-K-E."

T. J. rolled his eyes. "Mellow out, Albright. What are you gonna do, give out spelling demerits?"

"Well, I'm not voting for somebody who can't spell," Julie assured him.

"It's a play on words," said T. J. "*Salisbury Steak*— don't you get it?"

Joy nodded. "I get it, but it's dumb."

"I agree," said Julie. "It's like the election is just a big joke to him. If I were student body president, I know the first thing *I'd* do."

"Give everyone spelling tests?" asked T. J.

"Ha, ha, very funny," said Julie. "No—I'd change the detention system. No more writing stupid sentences a hundred times."

"Are you nuts?" asked T. J.

"I think it's a great idea," said Joy, her hands moving with her words. "You should run for school president. I'd vote for you."

"Have you two lost your marbles? You have to be in *sixth* grade to be student body president," T. J. pointed out.

"Says who?" Julie asked.

"I don't know—it's just the rule," said T. J.

"For your information, girls weren't allowed on the boys' basketball team, and I got *that* rule changed," Julie replied.

"Well, it wouldn't matter anyway," said T. J. "You'd never beat Mark Salisbury in a million years. He practically owns the school. He's as popular as the Fonz on *Happy Days*."

In spite of her annoyance, Julie smiled. *Happy Days* was a new TV series, and her sister Tracy had a crush on the Fonz.

"I still think you should run," said Joy. "I'll help you."

"Hey, you could be my vice president," said Julie. "We could run together. C'mon, Joy. Let's go ask the principal."

Julie clutched the red wooden hall pass a little too tightly as she and Joy stepped into the principal's office. Crossing the sea of gold carpet again reminded her of how scared she'd been the first time she had come to talk to Mr. Sanchez—about playing on the boys' basketball team. But when he stood up from behind his large wooden desk and greeted her with a smile, she instantly relaxed.

🌸 Poster Power 🌸

"Miss Albright," said Mr. Sanchez. "Are you getting ready for basketball season?"

Nodding her head, Julie held up the first finger on her right hand. "I hope I don't break my finger and miss the big game this year," she said.

Mr. Sanchez smiled. "I certainly hope not. And Miss Jenner, how are you liking fifth grade at Jack London?"

"So far so good," said Joy. "I'm getting a lot better at lip reading, and Julie helps me out."

"I'm glad to see you girls are friends. Now, what brings you here today?"

Julie took a deep breath. "Well, I'm thinking of running for student body president, but somebody said you have to be in sixth grade to run. Is that true?"

Mr. Sanchez raised his eyebrows. "As far as I know, there's no rule against a fifth grader running."

"Really?" Julie said, exchanging a hopeful glance with Joy.

"It's true that the student body president has always been a sixth grader," said the principal. "But you girls have as much right to run as anyone else."

"Can we put up posters in the hall, too?" Joy asked,

excitement written across her face.

"Yes, as long as you show them to Mr. Arnold first. He's in charge of student government."

"We're on our way to art class right now—maybe we can make our first poster," said Julie.

"I think this will be a good experience for you girls, and I wish you the best," said Mr. Sanchez, shaking their hands.

❀

"Mom!" Julie called, bursting through the door of Gladrags. Her mom's shop was a storefront below their second-story apartment. "Guess what! I'm going to run for school president."

Mom finished ringing up a sale, and then turned to Julie. "Hello to you, too, honey," she teased. "Take off your backpack and tell me everything."

In one breath, Julie told Mom about her exciting day. "I was wondering—can Joy come over? And is it okay to ask Ivy, too? I have to make a bunch of posters right away. The other guy already has his plastered all over the school."

"Posters sound like a great idea," said Mom. "There

are plenty of art supplies in back. And you could make popcorn for a snack. I'll be up in a little while."

"Yeah, a poster party! Thanks, Mom." Julie ran upstairs to call her friends.

An hour later, Julie's living room looked like a kindergarten class. Poster boards, markers, paints, scissors, and scraps of paper littered the couch, table, and floor. The three girls sat on the rug, bent over the posters.

"You sure get to do a lot of neat stuff at your school," Ivy remarked.

"Yeah, like detention," Julie joked, and the three girls fell into a fit of giggles.

"Ivy, we thought up a bunch of slogans, but would you mind doing the rest of the lettering? Mine's all crooked. Your printing's the best," Julie said, handing her a paintbrush.

"Sure, I love doing lettering," said Ivy.

"She doesn't even have to outline in pencil first," Julie told Joy.

For the next half hour, the only sound in the room was the friendly squeaking of markers and the snip of scissors as the three girls worked.

"How do these look?" Ivy asked, holding up a poster in each hand. *"Your future is bright with Albright,"* one poster proclaimed. *"Jump for Joy and Julie!"* said the other.

"They look great!" said Julie. She held up her own poster. "Your lettering is way better than mine."

"They look like works of art!" Joy said with admiration.

"Thanks," said Ivy, flashing a smile at Joy. "Here, now let's decorate them."

While Joy drew squiggles with glue, Julie dusted the glue with glitter.

Joy and Ivy pointed at Julie at the same time, giggling. "You've got green glitter all over your pants," Ivy laughed.

When the girls were finished, they stood up, brushing themselves off. They lined up the posters around the room and counted.

"We have ten posters," said Ivy.

"That's twice as many as Mark has up," said Joy.

"And they look three times as good!" Julie said with satisfaction.

On Thursday morning, Julie and Joy got to school early and proudly hung their posters in the hall, outside the library, and above the bleachers in the gym.

"What's all this?" asked T. J. as they were about to tape up the last poster above the fifth-grade lockers. "You can't be serious. You're really going to run for student body president against the most popular guy in the school?"

Julie and Joy exchanged a glance. "We're not afraid of that Mark guy," Joy declared.

"Besides, we have things we want to change about our school," Julie added.

"School elections aren't about changing stuff," said T. J. "They're about who's captain of the track team, or who has the most friends. It's a popularity contest. And Salisbury is *Mister* Popularity."

Julie rolled her eyes. "Are you going to stand there telling us how popular this Mark guy is, or are you going to use those hoopster arms to help us put up the last poster?"

"Okay, okay," said T. J. "Hand over the tape. But don't say I didn't warn you."

At lunchtime, Julie and Joy were waiting in the cafeteria line when T. J. rushed up to them. "Quick, you guys have to see this," he said urgently. The girls left their trays and ducked under the metal railing, following T. J. to the gym, where he pointed to their posters on the wall.

Julie gasped, charging up the bleachers to take a closer look. Someone had changed the name *Joy* to *Joke*. The word *vote* now read *vomit*. And there were big black mustaches on their school pictures.

"This is so mean," said Joy, slumping down onto the bleachers.

"Who would do something like this?" asked Julie, a flash of anger darkening her eyes.

"I bet I know *exactly* who did this," said T. J.

"You saw someone?" Joy asked, pointing to her eyes and signing while she spoke.

"Well, no, but at morning recess I heard Mark tell Jeff, his vice president, what a joke it is that you're running against him."

"A joke!" Julie sputtered. "What do you mean?"

"You know, because for one thing you're a fifth grader and for another thing, well, you're a girl." T. J. looked sheepish.

Julie glared at him. "What does being a girl have to do with it?"

"I'm just telling you what I heard," said T. J., holding up both hands defensively.

"What are we going to do now?" Joy asked. "These posters are wrecked. All that work for nothing."

"We could draw mustaches on Mark, too," T. J. suggested.

"No," said Julie. "For one thing, we don't know for sure if he's the one who did this. And besides, it's not right."

T. J. crossed his arms and stared hard at the posters, his eyes narrowing. "Well, whoever did this should get detention, that's for sure."

"Don't say *that*," Julie groaned. "That's what I'm trying to change." She ripped a poster down from the wall.

Joy started to pull down another poster, then stopped and looked at it thoughtfully. "We might be able to save these," she said slowly.

"How?" asked T. J. "Are you two going to grow mustaches?" He flashed a silly grin.

Joy smiled. "We can just glue new pictures on that one."

"But what about this one?" Julie asked. "It says *JOKE* in really big letters."

Joy studied the poster for a moment. "How about *Voting is no JOKE.*"

"Not bad," said Julie. "I like it."

T. J. held up the poster with the word *vomit*. "I know. How about *Mark is from Planet Vomit?*"

The girls laughed. "Well, at least the other side is blank," said Julie. "Let's make a new poster right now."

"But what about lunch?" T. J. asked.

"T. J., is food all you ever think about?" Julie asked as she rolled up the poster. "C'mon, Joy, let's go."

"Wait," said T. J. "Why don't we go eat real fast and then hit the art room during recess and fix these."

The girls paused. "You mean you're going to help us?" asked Joy.

"And you're actually giving up *recess*?" Julie asked.

"Sure, why not?" said T. J. "We can't let Mark get away with this."

Julie smiled. Deep down, she knew she could count on T. J.

"I can be like the guy that runs your campaign," T. J. continued. "I'll come up with good ideas—you know, help you from behind the scenes."

"You mean like a manager?" asked Joy. "For our campaign?"

"Yep," said T. J., tearing down the last of the posters. "Campaign manager," he said slowly. "I like it. Sounds official, don't you think?"

Julie reached over and gave T. J. an exaggerated handshake. "I think you've got yourself a deal!"

Julie for President

❧ CHAPTER 14 ❧

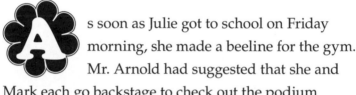s soon as Julie got to school on Friday morning, she made a beeline for the gym. Mr. Arnold had suggested that she and Mark each go backstage to check out the podium and test the microphone before the assembly.

Julie had never stood onstage in front of the whole school before. She'd have five minutes to talk about herself, her platform, and why she thought she would make a good student body president. Although she'd practiced the night before, just thinking about it made her stomach do a nervous, excited flip-flop.

Backstage, Julie dodged stacks of folding chairs and boxes of Drama Club props. She set her notes down on the podium and stood for a moment in the quiet dark. Closing her eyes, she imagined delivering her speech to an excited audience. Everybody hated demerits and feared detention, so she knew they would love her ideas. A shiver went up her spine—she could almost hear the clapping and cheering.

Just then, from behind the curtain, she heard voices. It sounded like the Water Fountain Girls—Angela, Amanda, and Alison, three girls from her class who were always hanging around the water fountain and talking about people in gossipy whispers.

"I can't believe he talked to us—fifth graders!" Amanda squealed.

"Where did he say to hang this poster?" Alison asked, her voice bubbling with excitement.

"Right in the center. That's where the podium will be," said Angela. "There—that looks perfect. I'm voting for him for sure."

"But what about Julie?" asked Alison. "After all, she's a fifth grader like us. Maybe we should—"

"I heard that he's going to get us a whole extra FREE DAY off from school," said Amanda.

"Sure, why not? If he can get a pool for our school, he can get a free day," Angela said confidently.

"A pool? Doesn't that cost tons of money?" asked Alison.

"Just think—we could have a swim team."

"And pool parties!" The girls squealed and giggled, jumping up and down.

"I feel kind of bad for Julie, though," said Alison. "She doesn't stand a chance."

"She might have half a chance if it weren't for that deaf girl running with her," Amanda said. "I mean, what was she thinking?"

Julie caught her breath, and her face turned hot. Just then, she heard footsteps behind her. *Joy.* Julie turned and put a finger to her lips, motioning for Joy to be quiet.

"Yeah, no one in their right mind's going to vote for her," said Angela. "She's always staring and waving her hands around like this." There was a pause, and the other two girls cackled. "And she sounds so weird when she talks."

"I know," Amanda agreed. "If Julie wants to get any votes at all, she better dump that deaf girl before the assembly. Once she opens her mouth, it's all over."

Julie's forehead felt as if it were on fire. She hoped it was too dark backstage for Joy to see her burning face.

"We'd better get to class," said Alison. "The bell's about to ring."

When Julie was sure the girls were gone, she burst through the curtain and jumped down off the stage to get a look at the poster they'd hung. Joy followed close behind. Julie couldn't look at her.

"What's wrong?" Joy asked. Her too-loud voice seemed to echo in the empty gym.

"Nothing," said Julie.

"It's those girls, isn't it?" Joy came close and touched Julie's hand. "Did they say something mean about you?"

Julie took a deep breath to calm herself. She couldn't bring herself to tell Joy they were saying mean things about *her*. But Joy read it in her face.

"Oh, I get it. They were talking about me, weren't they?" Joy asked. She was turning angry now—her hands flew in the air, signing forcefully along with each spoken word.

Clearing her throat, Julie tried to look casual. "Don't worry about them. They were just saying that we—we don't stand a chance against Mark."

"I know they don't like me," Joy said flatly. "It's because I'm deaf, isn't it?"

Julie turned to her friend, looking her straight in the eye. "I know it must be hard not being able to hear. But trust me, some things are better off not being heard."

No sooner was Julie back in class than she looked at her empty hands and realized she didn't have her note cards. In a panic, she tapped Joy and asked, "Did you see my note cards? Was I holding them when you came backstage?"

"No," Joy shook her head. "I didn't see them."

"I must have left them on the podium. I was going to practice, but then—" Julie paused, thinking. "Tell Mrs. Duncan I'll be back in a minute."

"But you'll be late—" Joy protested, pointing to the clock as Julie zoomed off down the hall.

Julie walked as fast as she could without running on her way to the gym. It was all she could do not to sprint. One thing she did not need was another demerit for running in the halls.

Rushing up the back steps onto the stage, she marched straight to the podium, but her note cards were nowhere to be seen. She looked all around the podium and on the floor around the stage, but it was no use. Her note cards were gone.

Mrs. Duncan tried to get the class to focus on Lewis and Clark, but the students were buzzing with excitement about the assembly. Julie sat silently, trying not to panic and wondering how she would give a speech without her notes. It was almost a relief when an announcement came over the loudspeaker and Mrs. Duncan told the class to line up by rows at the door.

On the way to the gym, Julie whispered to Joy, "What am I going to do?"

You've practiced that speech a million times. You know it by heart. You'll do great, Joy signed silently. Julie nodded to show Joy she understood, and smiled gratefully.

As the students took their seats, Mr. Arnold tapped the microphone. "Testing. Testing. Welcome, students, to the official kickoff of the 1976 election for student body president. As most of you know, this November our country will be electing a new president of the United States. And we here at Jack London Elementary are electing a new school president. Today, we'll get a chance to hear from the candidates. First up will be sixth grader Mark Salisbury."

The audience went wild. Sixth graders stomped their feet, rattling the bleachers and yelling, "Go, Mark! Yahoo!"

Mark stepped up to the podium. He took out his note cards, tapped them on the podium, and cleared his throat.

"Fellow students, I know you don't want to listen to a long boring speech with lots of promises, so I promise to make this short and sweet. One word will sum up my platform." He leaned in toward the microphone. "Pizza!"

The audience clapped and cheered.

"If I am elected president," Mark went on, "I promise to get pizza every Friday for hot lunch in the cafeteria. No more mystery meat and stewed tomatoes." Then Mark clapped his hands together and started a chant, "Piz-za Fri-day, Piz-za Fri-day," and soon he had nearly all the students clapping and chanting. Mark stepped away from the podium and took several dramatic bows, hamming it up for the audience.

Pizza? That's why he's running for school president? Julie thought to herself, but she looked out at the other students and saw that they were completely swept up in the moment. Her stomach did a nervous cartwheel. All of a sudden, the speech she had prepared seemed much too serious. Maybe she should just scrap the whole thing and think up a catchy word or gimmick, as Mark had. But it was too late. Mark was already passing her on the stage, taking his seat.

"Forget your note cards, Albright?" Mark said under his breath. So Mark must have found her note cards after she checked the podium, and taken them! T. J. was right—Mark really was a sleazeball. She couldn't just let him win. Julie sat with her hands clenched in her lap, hoping to steady herself as Mr. Arnold introduced her.

"... and we thought Mark was going to run unopposed, but fifth grader Julie Albright has decided to make this a real contest. So let's give a warm welcome to Julie Albright."

Several students clapped politely, but there were no hoots or hollers as there had been for Mark. A hiss of "fifth grader" went through the sixth-grade bleachers.

Julie longed for her note cards, just to have something to hold on to. As she stepped up to the podium, she reminded herself why she was running—because of something she believed in. Because she wanted to make her school a better place.

"Principals, teachers, and fellow students," Julie began, suddenly thinking of a good way to start her speech. "I like pizza as much as anybody, but today I'm here to talk to you about something that affects us all—detention."

"Bor-ing," a boy in the back row called out.

Swallowing hard, Julie plunged ahead. She briefly outlined her plan to do away with detention and demerits.

The gymnasium grew dead quiet. Students looked sideways at teachers, not sure how to react, as though they might get in trouble for just thinking about the idea. Then a group of sixth-grade boys, led by Stinger, began hooting and stomping at the top of the bleachers. Stinger started his own chant, "Down with detention! Down with detention!" but it quickly fizzled out.

Julie nervously brushed back her hair, shifting from foot to foot. "What I mean to say is, instead of sitting in detention writing sentences over and over, we could be doing something positive for our school." She looked out at the audience. Hundreds of eyes stared blankly at her.

She raised her voice a notch. "Um, we could scrub graffiti off the bathroom walls. Or plant flowers, or pick up litter—stuff like that." Still no reaction. The bright spotlight glared down on her. Julie wiped beads of sweat from her forehead. She couldn't for the life of her remember how her speech ended. Hurriedly thanking the audience, she sat down. A few weak claps here and there seemed to mock her.

Mr. Arnold thanked her and made some final remarks. Julie didn't hear them. She fixed her eyes on the plaid pattern of his shirt and willed herself not to cry.

When Julie got home from school that day, she dragged herself into the apartment, dropped her backpack, and slumped onto the couch.

"How did your speech go today, honey?" Mom asked, exchanging glances with Tracy.

"Not too good, from the looks of it," said Tracy as she headed into the kitchen for a snack.

Mom put down her laundry basket and sat next

to Julie on the couch. "Tell me about it, honey."

"It was a disaster." Julie explained about her missing note cards, Mark and his Pizza Fridays, and the silent reaction she'd gotten to her ideas. "The bad kids were the only ones who liked it!"

"You still have more than a week to go before the election," said Mom. "Anything can happen in politics. Look at Jimmy Carter. Everybody loved him after the Democratic convention this summer, and they were upset with Ford because he pardoned Nixon after Watergate."

"But I thought Nixon lied," said Julie.

"That's why a lot of people started looking at Carter. Then Carter announced that he would pardon all the Vietnam War draft dodgers—those young men who left the country rather than fight in a war they didn't believe in," Mom explained. "Now it's a much closer race."

Tracy poked her head out of the kitchen doorway. "My civics teacher said he admires Carter for having the courage to say what he believes is right, even though it's unpopular."

"See?" said Mom. "Carter may lose votes over his ideas, but he'll gain some, too. Look at Hank. He told

me he's voting for Carter because he thinks the war
was wrong, and he's a Vietnam veteran."

"Who are you going to vote for, Mom?" Julie asked.

"I'm going to vote for Jimmy Carter," Mom told
her. "I like his ideas, and I think this country needs a
change."

Julie nodded. "That's what I'm trying to do for our
school—make a change."

But even as she said the words, Julie knew it
wouldn't be as simple as she had thought. She remembered last year when she had tried to join the boys'
basketball team. "Any time you try to change something, it's going to be difficult," her mom had warned,
and she had been right.

Change had been hard to accept in her own life
after her parents' divorce. It had taken time to get used
to, and she'd had to find a new way of thinking about
her family. Julie realized that if she wanted people to
be open to her ideas, she would have to give them a
new way to look at detention—a new way of thinking
about it. But how?

Mom handed Julie a pile of folded laundry. "Here,
honey—some clean clothes if you want to take them to

Dad's this weekend. You'd better get packed. He'll be here any minute."

That evening after dinner, while Julie helped Dad with the dishes, she asked, "Dad, are you going to vote for Carter or Ford for president?"

"Well, I'll tell you, I've been thinking a lot about this," Dad said, looking up from scraping the bottom of the pot roast pan. "Right now, I'm planning to vote for President Ford."

"But what about Carter?"

"Carter seems like a decent man, but we just don't know much about him," Dad answered. "And I'm not sure this country is ready for some of his new ideas. Americans have been through a lot in the past few years. I think it might be better to stick with a familiar president who knows how to run the country."

Julie dried off a dinner plate and stacked it in the cupboard. "Do you think you might change your mind?" she asked him.

"Well, so far there's been only one debate on TV, and I think Ford came out ahead on that one. But there's another debate next week, right here in San Francisco in fact, and I'll be watching it to hear what both candidates have to say."

Julie stopped drying the bowl in her hand. "How come the debates are so important?"

"In a debate, you get a much better idea of what the candidates think on all kinds of issues," Dad explained, handing the pot roast pan over to Julie. "Tell you what—if you're interested, I'll come pick you up and we can watch the debates together."

"Really? That would be groovy," said Julie, feeling very grown-up. Tracy and her teenage friends often said *groovy*. Julie finished drying the pan and hung up her damp towel. "And you know what, Dad? This just gave me a great idea for my campaign."

Heating Up

n Monday morning, Julie and Mark had a meeting with Mr. Arnold. Julie suggested a debate between the candidates.

"I think that's a great idea, Julie," said the vice principal. But Mark looked shocked.

"You want me to debate a *girl*?" Mark said, as if Julie weren't even in the room. He put his hands on his hips. "Is there any rule that says I have to?"

"There's no rule," said Mr. Arnold. "But it would be a great opportunity for the students to get to know the candidates better."

"They already know *me*," said Mark.

"All they know is that you want pizza for school lunch," said Julie. "This would give us a chance to debate other issues we care about."

Mark wouldn't look at Julie. "Why should I help

her?" he asked Mr. Arnold. "She already knows she's going to lose."

"I'm sorry you see it that way, Mark," said Mr. Arnold. "I think a debate would be a terrific experience. I'd like you to think it over."

"Sorry," said Mark, turning to go. "Not interested."

As Julie headed down the hall toward her locker, she felt disappointment dragging her steps. Earlier that morning, she'd jumped out of bed, excited about the possibility of a debate. But Mark had burst her bubble, and she was back to feeling helpless and frustrated.

"You look like we just lost a basketball game or something," said T. J. He and Joy were standing near Julie's locker, waiting for her.

As they headed to class, Julie started to tell her friends about the debate.

"Whoa," said T. J., his face lighting up. "That's a great idea."

"You're brave," said Joy. "It would be hard to get up in front of all those people again and debate Mark."

"Doesn't matter," Julie sighed. "Mark said no."

T. J. stopped in his tracks. "What do you mean he said no?"

Julie shrugged. "He knows he's going to win, so why should he debate me?"

"If he's so sure, then why's he afraid to debate you?" T. J. asked.

"He doesn't want to, and he doesn't have to," said Julie.

"We just have to think up another way to get our ideas across," said Joy.

"Maybe this'll help," said T. J. He reached into his backpack and pulled out two buttons that said *NO DETENTION*.

"You made these?" asked Joy. "For us?"

"My dad has a button-making machine," said T. J. "I was thinking you guys could wear these. You'll be like walking ads. Maybe it'll help get your ideas out."

"Wow," said Julie, pinning her button to her sweater. "Thanks, T. J."

"Hey, what are campaign managers for?" He bobbed his head, a hunk of sandy hair flopping over his eyes, and smiled ear to ear.

"I have an idea," said Joy. "Maybe we could stand

by the front door after school and talk to kids as they get on their buses. We can wear our buttons and tell them about changing the detention system."

"Brilliant," Julie said, grinning.

When the day was over and the final bell rang, Julie and Joy headed down to the front lobby. Kids started pouring down the halls and out the front door.

"No more detention," Julie called out as kids filed past her. "Vote for Julie. Change the system."

Kids hurried past her, eager to get to their buses. *Nobody's even listening,* thought Julie. She peeled one of their posters off the wall and turned to Joy. "Here, hold this poster out so all the kids will see it, while I do the talking."

Julie went up to a group of kids and asked them what they thought about demerits and detention. The students stared silently at her. Nervously, she glanced at Joy. Joy stood stiffly, barely holding up the poster.

A boy in a red jacket bumped into Joy and gave her an unfriendly look. "Hey, watch out. You're blocking the way."

"Joy," said Julie impatiently, "why are you just standing there? Can't you hold up the poster like I said?"

Joy let the poster drop. As she spoke, her hands flew so fast, Julie had to step back to get out of the way. *I may be deaf, but I can still speak for myself.*

"Sorry," said Julie. "I didn't mean—never mind. Don't worry about the poster. Let's both talk to as many kids as we can. There's not much time before the buses leave."

Joy stood by the other set of doors. "Hi, I'm Joy Jenner," she started, but Julie watched the kids brush right past her. "Vote for Julie for school president," Joy tried again. The kids began heading out the opposite door to avoid walking past her.

"Who is that girl, anyway?" asked a girl in a corduroy jumper.

"When she talks, she sounds like she's inside a fishbowl," said another.

"Maybe her name's Flipper!" said a boy, and he began singing the *Flipper* theme song all the way to the bus. *"They call her Flipper, Flipper, faster than lightning ..."*

Julie crumpled inside. She had known that the other

kids thought Joy was weird, strange, different. What she hadn't realized—until now, seeing it with her own eyes—was that this made them a little bit afraid of her.

Watching the kids skirt around Joy to the other exit, Julie suddenly felt dizzy with uncertainty. She knew it wouldn't be right to ask Joy not to speak up for herself. But Julie had to admit that when Joy did speak, it made things worse. The truth was, having Joy for a vice president was ruining any chance she had at being elected student body president—or even at getting kids to think about her ideas. But how on earth could she tell her friend that?

When the final bus pulled away from the curb, Julie couldn't help feeling relieved. The girls began walking home in silence.

"Want to come walk the dogs with me today?" Joy finally asked when they got to Belvedere Street.

"I—I can't, not today. Sorry," Julie stammered. Feeling guilty, she rushed off toward home.

Julie dropped her backpack inside the front door and went straight to her room, fighting back tears. A few minutes later, she heard Tracy yell, "Hey, why'd you dump your stuff in the middle of the doorway? I almost tripped and broke my—" But when Tracy got to Julie's room and saw her sister's face, she stopped.

"Jules?" she asked softly. "Are you okay?"

Julie didn't answer. Tracy sat down on the bed next to her. "Did something happen at school? Do you want to talk about it?"

"It's the election," Julie said dully. "Nobody gets my ideas, and Mark, the guy I'm running against, won't even be in a debate with me. Then today, when Joy and I tried to talk to kids about our ideas, everybody acted like we had major cooties."

"Cooties?" Tracy asked, trying to hold back a little smile.

"It's not funny!" said Julie. "It's like they think Joy has a disease and they're afraid they'll catch it. They look at her like she's weird. They call her names and say awful stuff about her, and she can't even hear them."

"I know—kids can be so mean," said Tracy. "In high school, some people are mean if they think you wear the wrong clothes." She reached over and smoothed out the bedspread between them.

"It's all a huge mess," Julie moaned. "I hate to say it, but I even started thinking maybe I should ask T. J. to run with me instead. I don't have a chance of winning with Joy as my vice president. Of course, I probably wouldn't win anyway. And I don't want to lose her as a friend." With a groan, Julie fell back on her bed. "Why did I ever think running for student body president was a good idea? It's the worst idea I've ever had."

The next morning, when Julie and Joy passed through the front doors of the school, they stopped, stunned.

Mark and Jeff stood at the front door, shaking hands with kids as they poured off the buses and headed for their classrooms. "I'm Mark Salisbury, your next student body president," Mark said, smiling with a big, toothy grin.

"He stole our idea!" said Joy.

Julie nodded but didn't say a word.

At their lockers, Julie turned to Joy. "We might as well admit it—Mark has us beat. He's going to win by a landslide. Let's just drop out of the race now and not give that Pizza Monster the satisfaction of eating us alive." Julie forced herself to meet Joy's eyes.

Joy looked surprised. She searched Julie's face. "That's not like you to quit," Joy said finally.

"I know, but—well, nothing has turned out the way I expected. It just seems like dropping out is the best thing to do now." *Please don't make this harder than it already is,* Julie begged silently.

"It's me, isn't it?" Joy looked at the floor. "I may be deaf, but I'm not blind. Nobody likes me. I'm the one they avoid. They don't even give you a chance because of me."

Julie buried her head in her locker so that Joy wouldn't see the truth of it on her face.

"If anybody drops out, it should be me," Joy went on. "You can ask T. J. to be your vice president. He's on the basketball team with you, and everybody likes him. But most of all, he's not deaf."

Julie wanted to protest, but instead she heard herself mumble, "Um, the bell's about to ring. We'd better get to class."

❀

Mrs. Duncan called on her twice that morning, and Julie fumbled through her notebook to find the right answers. She willed herself to sit up and pay attention to Lewis and Clark's ongoing journey. And Julie had to admit it *was* a pretty exciting journey. They had faced wild bears and raging rivers and long months of hardship. It reminded Julie of her wagon train trip last summer for the Bicentennial, although she knew Lewis and Clark's journey had been a lot more dangerous.

"'Courage undaunted, possessing a firmness and perseverance of purpose,'" said Mrs. Duncan. "That's how Thomas Jefferson described Lewis. What did he mean by that?"

The students squirmed in their seats, looking blankly back at the teacher. Slowly, one hand rose.

"Joy?" said Mrs. Duncan.

"I think he meant that Lewis was brave," Joy said slowly in her odd voice, "and that he didn't give up." She glanced sideways at Julie.

Julie blinked in surprise. Joy almost never spoke up in class. Was her friend trying to send her a message?

At lunch, T. J. practically tripped over himself racing up to Julie and Joy. "You're not going to believe this," he said, cutting in line next to them. "Did you see the signs I put up this morning that say 'Where's the Debate?' Everybody's buzzing about it—and now they want a debate."

"What?" Joy asked.

"Are you serious?" Julie asked.

T. J. nodded. "Get this—Jeff, Mark's own vice president, asked him why he's afraid to debate a girl. And guess what? Mark didn't know what to say, so he finally agreed to do it. You got your debate!"

"Too bad somebody's dropping out of the election," said Joy.

"What? Who—you?" T. J. asked, looking from Joy to Julie.

"I didn't say it was for sure," said Julie defensively. She couldn't admit that she'd been thinking about letting Joy drop out.

"You can't quit now," said T. J. "The election's just heating up!"

T. J. and Joy were right—she couldn't quit now. Julie firmly grasped her lunch tray and tossed back her hair, as if to shake off any lingering doubts about running with Joy or dropping out of the race.

"D-Day," T. J. said, coming up to Julie in the hall on Thursday morning.

"Huh?" Julie turned and gave him a blank look.

"Debate Day." He elbowed her in the ribs good-naturedly.

Julie bit her bottom lip. Now that the debate was here, her stomach fluttered with nervous anticipation. But she reminded herself that this was the best way to get her ideas across, and that steadied her.

When it was time for the debate, Julie took her place onstage at a podium opposite Mark. She stood squinting in the bright spotlight, looking out over the rows of students until she spotted Joy and T. J. in the audience. He had told her it might help to fix her eyes on a friendly face or two at first.

Mr. Arnold gave a short introduction, explaining the ground rules and time limits of the debate. He would ask a question, and each candidate would have a turn to answer. "Please hold your applause until the very end," said Mr. Arnold. "Now, first question: Why is student government important? Miss Albright, we'll begin with you."

Leaning in to the microphone, Julie said, "Student government is important because it gives all of us a say in what happens at our school."

"Mr. Salisbury?"

"Student government is important because we get to plan fun activities, like going to Marine World."

The crowd clapped and cheered, and Mr. Arnold had to remind them to hold their applause.

"Julie," said Mr. Arnold, glancing at his index cards, "Mark has proposed Pizza Fridays as his platform. Tell us what you think of his idea."

"Pizza's great!" said Julie. "I just think there are more important things to work on, like changing the detention system."

"Thank you, Julie. Mr. Salisbury, your comments on Julie's idea to change the detention system?"

"She doesn't know what she's talking about," said Mark.

"Yes I do," said Julie. "I've *been* to detention." The crowd laughed. "That's how I know we need to change it."

"Julie, I'm going to have to ask you to wait your turn to speak," Mr. Arnold cautioned.

"Sorry," said Julie, blushing and stepping away from the podium.

"If we didn't have detention," said Mark, "then all the bullies could do whatever they wanted, and the bad kids would take over the school. Everybody knows that. Or at least by the time you get to sixth grade, you do. Think about it—do you really want a student body president and vice president who have both been in detention?"

"Mr. Arnold," said Julie, raising her hand. "May I say one more thing?"

Mr. Arnold looked at his watch. "I'll allow a rebuttal. You have one minute."

Julie took a deep breath. The audience was silent, watching. And listening. "Of course if a student does something wrong, there has to be a consequence," she began. "But I don't see how sitting in detention and writing a sentence over and over a hundred times helps anybody. What I am saying is if we break a rule, we should make up for it by doing something good, instead of something useless that just gives you writer's cramp."

"Your one minute is up," said Mr. Arnold. "Mark, you have one minute to reply."

"Detention isn't supposed to be fun," said Mark. "It's supposed to be a punishment."

"But we should learn from our mistakes," said Julie. "And I think we'd learn more if we did something useful. Something that helps the whole school."

To Julie's surprise, the students burst into applause. Mr. Arnold had to quiet them down once more.

"Okay, let's move on," said Mr. Arnold. "Final question: If for some reason you had to leave the office of student body president, your vice president would take your place. Please tell us what qualifies him or her for this position. Mark?"

"Easy," said Mark. "My VP, Jeff Coopersmith, is captain of the crossing guards. Everybody knows him, and he's real tall so it would be easy to find him when you need him." Everyone laughed.

"Thank you, Mark. Julie, can you tell us what

qualifies your vice president to hold the office of student body president?"

Julie froze. The whole audience seemed to hold its breath, and for one long, awkward moment, all eyes were on Julie, waiting.

In the vast quiet, Julie heard herself begin to talk. "My vice president, Joy Jenner, is new to our school. Because she's new, many of you haven't gotten to know her. Instead of speaking for her, I'd like to ask her to come up to the podium and speak for herself."

In utter silence, all heads turned to watch Joy as she walked down the center aisle and up onto the stage. Julie stepped back from the microphone. Joy gripped the sides of the podium, as if steadying herself in a strong wind. Her eyelids fluttered and she took in a deep breath. When she opened her mouth, nothing came out.

Julie reached over and gave Joy's hand a soft squeeze. The whole audience seemed to sit closer, leaning in to hear Joy's words.

"I know I'm different," Joy started. "I know I talk funny. I can't hear what you hear because I'm deaf. But everybody feels different sometimes. And even though

I'm deaf, I promise to listen to you. I hope you'll give me a chance."

Wow! Great job, Julie signed to Joy while Mr. Arnold thanked everyone and wrapped up the assembly.

As Julie's class headed down the hall to their classroom, Mrs. Duncan lingered to congratulate the girls. "Julie, you did us proud in Room 5D." Julie beamed at the rare praise from her teacher. Then Mrs. Duncan turned to Joy. "Joy, I know it was difficult for you to speak in front of the whole school, but you really shined."

"Thanks," said Joy. She touched a hand to her chin, signing *thank you* with a shy smile.

As they approached their classroom, Julie heard a commotion inside. Through the open door, she could see the Water Fountain Girls standing in front of the whole class. Alison was holding out a bottle of glue like a microphone, and Amanda was speaking into it using a loud, nasal voice to imitate Joy at the podium during the debate. Angela was flailing her arms about in mock sign language.

"What in the world!" Mrs. Duncan barked. The three girls turned, red-faced. Marching into the classroom, Mrs. Duncan blinked the lights on and off, clapping sharply to get the class settled down. "Class! That is e-nough," she said, each syllable as sharp as her clapping. "At this school, we respect others, despite our differences."

In horror, Julie glanced at Joy. Joy's face twisted with pain, and she rushed off down the hall. "Joy, wait up," Julie called, hurrying after her. But her words just echoed down the empty corridor, unheard.

Julie found Joy crumpled on the floor in a corner of the girls' bathroom. She knelt beside her on the cold tile and gently put a hand on Joy's shoulder.

Finally, Joy raised her tear-stained face. "I did my best, but it wasn't enough. They think I'm stupid—stupid like a clown." She put her head in her arms and sobbed.

Julie swallowed, feeling her eyes well with sympathy. She didn't know what she could say to help Joy feel better. Finally, she tapped Joy on the shoulder to get her attention. "Last year, when I was the new girl, those same girls said mean stuff about me, too. I know how you feel." But even as Julie spoke the words, she wasn't so sure. It was one thing to have the Water Fountain Girls talk about you behind your back in the halls or at the water fountain. It was another thing for them to make fun of someone in front of the whole class.

Joy shook her head and looked away. "I can't go back there, ever."

"Joy, listen—you can't hide in the girls' bathroom forever. Pretty soon the lunch bell will ring and there'll be a ton of kids in here."

Joy pulled herself up. "I don't feel so good," she said, clutching her knees.

Julie put her arm around Joy. "C'mon, I'll walk you to the nurse's office."

❀

When Julie got back to class, Mrs. Duncan stepped out into the hall with her. "Where's Joy? Is she all right?"

Julie shook her head. "She has a stomach ache, so she's lying down in the nurse's office."

Mrs. Duncan rubbed her forehead. "I'll check on her later. Let's give her some time to herself. It was terribly hurtful what those girls did. They will have to apologize to Joy."

Julie nodded and headed back to her seat. She

flushed as she felt eyes on her, and she stared straight ahead at her desk to avoid making eye contact with the Water Fountain Girls. The empty desk beside her seemed to announce its presence. Julie tried to concentrate on her math worksheet, but none of the columns seemed to add up.

Julie stared at the Sloppy Joe on her lunch tray. She hadn't touched a bite of her food.

T. J. plopped his tray down next to Julie's. "Boy oh boy, I've never seen Duncan Donut so mad. When you and Joy were gone, she really blasted those girls. You should have seen it. She was practically spitting when she gave them detention."

Julie looked up from her tray. "They got detention?"

"More like triple detention. They have to write 'I will not make fun of others' three hundred times. That's like six pages front and back!"

"Oh, no." Julie put her head in her hands.

"What!? They deserve it!" T. J. said heatedly. "You guys were boss in that debate. You beat the pants off Mark, and all they did was make fun of you." He took a big bite of his Sloppy Joe.

"That's not the point, T. J.," Julie moaned.

"Listen, Julie," T. J. said with his mouth full. "I know you're against detention, but this time they really deserve it."

Julie hated to admit it, but part of her just wanted to see the Water Fountain Girls punished.

T. J. leaned across the table toward her. "Are you saying they should get away with it?"

Julie shook her head. It was starting to ache. She took a sip of her chocolate milk.

"Well?" T. J. asked, still waiting for an answer.

"T. J., if those girls do a dumb detention where they write the same sentence a million times, how will that help anything? Will it make them sorry for what they did? You know it won't—it'll just make them hate Joy more than ever. After all, if it wasn't for her, they wouldn't be stuck in detention in the first place. That's how they'll see it."

"I guess," T. J. shrugged. "That's just how kids are."

"And that's why detention doesn't work."

"Well, okay then, Miss Smartypants—if you were Mrs. Duncan, what would *you* do?"

Julie rubbed her forehead. "I'm not sure."

"Good thing it's not up to you, then," said T. J. "Hey, can I have your Sloppy Joe if you're not going to eat it?"

Julie pushed it toward him. "Here." She got up. "I'm going to see how Joy's doing."

But when she got to the nurse's office, the cot was empty, and the nurse told Julie that Joy had gone home.

The Election

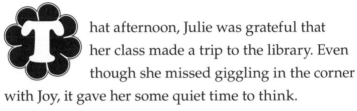 hat afternoon, Julie was grateful that her class made a trip to the library. Even though she missed giggling in the corner with Joy, it gave her some quiet time to think.

Her thoughts were in a tangle. As much as she wanted to see the Water Fountain Girls pay for what they'd done, she knew in her heart that detention wasn't the answer. Writing sentences wouldn't change the Water Fountain Girls at all, or make school better for Joy.

But what *was* the answer?

Julie fiddled with the macramé key chain on the end of her house key, twisting and untwisting the knots and loose ends. Over and over in her head she heard T. J.'s words—*If you were Mrs. Duncan, what would you do?*

Julie looked around the library, groping for an idea. Her eyes landed on the familiar Dewey Decimal poster, the beanbag pillow on the floor of the story corner, the stuffed animals lining the tops of the low shelves. She scanned the spines of the books against the back wall. Biographies. *Anne Frank: The Diary of a Young Girl. And Then What Happened, Paul Revere?* She stared at the shelves directly in front of her. The 400s. Languages. *How to Speak Spanish.*

Languages. It was as if Joy spoke a foreign language, one that the Water Fountain Girls did not understand.

But what if they could speak her language? Maybe if they got to know Joy, they wouldn't act so cruel.

"Last call for checking out books," called Mrs. Paterson, the librarian, startling Julie out of her deep thought.

Julie hopped up. There *was* a book she wanted to check out, if she could find the right one. Running her fingers along the spines, she saw it: *Sign Language Is Fun.* She took it to the checkout desk.

"Going to learn some sign language, Julie?" asked Mrs. Paterson.

"You know my friend Joy Jenner?" Julie asked. "She already taught me some signs, but I want to learn some new signs to surprise her."

"Good for you," said Mrs. Paterson, stamping the

date due card and sliding it back into the pocket.

As Julie headed back to class, she flipped through the book thoughtfully. *Poster. President. School.* This book had all the signs she would need.

Suddenly, she knew how to answer T. J.'s question. Now she just had to get Mrs. Duncan to go along with her idea.

The final bell rang. While the other students hurriedly gathered their books and clunked their chairs upside-down on their desks, the Water Fountain Girls dragged themselves out the door and off to detention.

"Mrs. Duncan?" Julie asked, hugging her books to her chest as she approached the teacher's desk. "May I ask you a question?"

"What is it, Julie?" Mrs. Duncan sounded tired.

"Mrs. Duncan," Julie repeated, "I know what those girls did was wrong, and they hurt Joy a lot. But I've been thinking—um, well, how is writing sentences going to help them to learn from what they did or make them act better in the future?"

"I'm not sure what you're suggesting, Julie. I know

you have a low opinion of detention, but it will force those girls to write and think about what they've done."

"Will it?" asked Julie. "Just look at Stinger—detention doesn't seem to be making *him* act any better. Last year, you gave him forty-three detentions, and he hasn't changed one bit."

"Well, I'll give you that," said Mrs. Duncan, gathering up the folders on her desk and sliding them into her tote bag. "All right, Julie. Go ahead—tell me what you're thinking."

Julie held up her library book for Mrs. Duncan to see. "I was thinking I could teach them some sign language."

Mrs. Duncan's eyes widened with surprise, but Julie kept right on talking. "Joy taught me lots of signs, and I'm learning even more from this book. Maybe if they learned some sign language, it would help them understand Joy a little better, and they wouldn't feel like she's so weird or different anymore . . ." Julie stopped twisting the hem of her shirt and looked anxiously at Mrs. Duncan. Was her teacher angry with her?

Mrs. Duncan was quiet. She shuffled some papers on her desk. She picked up her calendar book and put it in her bag. Julie felt certain that the creases in her teacher's forehead were disapproving.

After what felt like forever, Mrs. Duncan set down her tote bag. She looked up at Julie and said, "You know what? Maybe this is worth a try." She scribbled out a note and handed it to Julie. "Go on down to the library and give this note to Mr. Arnold. Ask the girls to come back to the classroom. I can stay an extra hour today."

"Really? You mean it?" Julie let out a breath. "Thank you, Mrs. Duncan."

"No, thank you," said Mrs. Duncan. "After twenty-three years of teaching, I just might be learning something new."

The Water Fountain Girls were leery as they followed Julie back to the classroom.

"What did you pull us out of detention for?" Angela huffed.

"We weren't even half done writing our sentences. You better not be getting us in more trouble," said Amanda.

"You want to go back there?" Julie snapped. "Go

right ahead—be my guest. Excuse me for thinking maybe you'd rather do something besides write a million sentences till your hands fall off. Not that you don't deserve it."

"What do you mean?" Alison asked.

"Are you saying you're going to get us out of writing all those sentences?" asked Angela. "Why would you be nice to us? What's the catch?"

Julie glared at her. "All you think about are yourselves. Did you ever stop to think for one minute about Joy—that I might be doing something for *her*, not for you?"

As Julie explained her idea, Angela rolled her eyes and Amanda stood with her hand on her hip. Alison just stared at the floor. When Julie was finished, there was a long, uncomfortable silence.

Finally Alison looked up at her friends. "Well, at least this sounds better than detention."

"I guess," said Amanda reluctantly.

"It's not like we really have a choice," Angela muttered as they followed Julie into Mrs. Duncan's room.

Alison, Amanda, and Angela pulled their chairs to form a semicircle around Julie. She started out by helping each girl create a unique sign for her name.

Then she showed them a few simple signs, like *hello* and *please*. Next, Julie looked up signs in her library book for things around the room—clock, window, desk, hamster—and showed them how to make the hand signs.

"This is hard," Angela grumbled. "I can't make my fingers work right."

"I'll teach you how to finger-spell," Julie said. Soon she, Alison, Amanda, and Angela were singing "A-B-C-D-E-F-G," moving their hands in time to the song and trying to remember the finger positions for each letter. They ran through the song a few times, faster and faster, and ended breathless and laughing.

"I never in a million years thought I'd be singing the alphabet song in fifth grade!" Alison exclaimed.

"My fingers are all tangled up," Amanda said with a giggle.

Even Angela cracked a small smile.

"Girls, I'm afraid that's all the time we have for today," said Mrs. Duncan.

The four girls were quiet as they put their chairs back up onto the desks and gathered their books and belongings.

Alison leaned on the rungs of her upside-down chair

for a moment and breathed a heavy sigh. "Julie?" she started softly. "Does this mean you're not mad at us?"

Julie hesitated for a moment. Then she rubbed her thumb against her index finger.

"What does that mean?" Alison asked.

"A little bit," Julie said.

Alison looked grateful and gave her a quick smile.

Amanda had edged closer. Suddenly she blurted out, "Do you think Joy will ever forgive us for what we did?"

"I don't know," Julie answered.

Alison spoke up again. "Before we go, will you show us how to sign the word *sorry*?"

"Okay, sure," said Julie. "First, make the letter *A*." She held out a fist with her thumb facing up. "Then rub it in a circle over your heart."

All three girls watched Julie intently. Then, carefully, they formed their hands into the letter *A* and made circles over their hearts.

On Friday morning, when Julie arrived at school, Amanda, Alison, and Angela were waiting inside the front lobby. They rushed up to her.

"Where's Joy?" Angela demanded.

"She's coming today, right?" asked Amanda.

Julie shook her head. "I stopped by her house on the way to school, but her mother said she still isn't feeling well."

"But it's Friday—that means we won't see her until Monday," said Alison, looking distressed.

The three girls exchanged a glance.

"We can't wait till Monday," said Angela. "We have to tell her we're sorry."

"We *want* to tell her," Alison added.

Julie shifted her backpack, thinking.

"Hey, Julie," said Amanda, "do you think we could have detention again today?"

"Huh?" Julie asked. "You mean—"

"Yeah, you know, stay after school, like yesterday, and learn more signs," Amanda explained.

Julie looked up, startled, and then broke into a grin. "Oh, so you think my idea for changing detention is better than Pizza Fridays?"

The three girls looked sheepish at first. Then Angela looked up. "Well, duh!" she said, and all four girls laughed.

"Tell you what," said Julie. "Why don't we hold detention at Joy's house after school today. Maybe we can cheer her up."

After school, the four girls walked to Joy's house. Julie rang the bell, which made a light flash inside the house for Joy to see. Amanda hung back, and Alison and Angela shuffled nervously behind Julie.

Joy opened the door. "Julie! Come on in. What are you—" Then her face went white as she saw the other girls. She stood stiffly, with the door half-open.

"It's okay," said Julie, reaching for Joy's hand. Joy pulled back as if she'd been burned.

"Joy, please let us in," said Angela, stepping forward. "We just want to talk to you."

"We came to say we're sorry," said Alison, rubbing her heart with her fist. Angela and Amanda quickly joined in.

Joy's dark eyes welled up as she opened the door wider.

Sitting on the floor around the coffee table in the front room, the Water Fountain Girls told Joy how sorry they were. Julie could see in their faces that they meant it, and she knew Joy could see it, too.

Joy's mother came in with mugs of hot chocolate, and soon the room was filled with chatter and signing.

"What I don't get is how did the three of you learn all this sign language?" asked Joy, her forehead crinkling.

Julie told Joy about the new detention.

"And it really worked!" said Alison and Angela at the same time. All the girls laughed.

When it was time to go, the girls brought their mugs into the kitchen and thanked Mrs. Jenner.

On their way out the door, Alison turned to Julie. "What's the sign for *friend*?"

Julie showed her how to hook index fingers to say *friend* in sign language. Alison reached over and hooked her finger with Joy's. As they locked fingers together, a fleeting trace of a smile passed over Joy's face, like sun peeking through a cloud.

On Monday morning, Julie and Joy walked to school together. Even though it was election day and Julie was anxious, at least Joy was back at school. No matter what happened, they'd face it together.

As they entered the school, Julie saw T. J. at the edge of a crowd of students. He waved, but instead of coming over, he turned and called, "They're here!" The crowd parted, and there in the middle of the front lobby stood the Water Fountain Girls, dressed from head to toe in green and blue, the school colors.

"From the top. One, two, three!" called Angela as she, Amanda, and Alison led the crowd in a song:

> *If you're happy and you know it,*
> *vote for Julie.*
> *If you're happy and you know it,*
> *jump for Joy.*
> *If you're happy and you know it,*
> *Then your VOTE will really show it.*
> *If you're happy and you know it . . .*
> *VOTE FOR JULIE! JUMP FOR JOY!*

Everybody clapped and cheered.

Joy touched the tips of both hands to her mouth and extended them out in gratitude, signing *thank you* to the three girls.

"Wow, thanks, you guys!" said Julie. "That was really neat."

"Yeah, I wish I'd thought of it," said T. J., "but they came up with it on their own. Isn't it great? Now lots of people are saying they're going to vote for you guys."

Julie looked around. Students were humming the catchy tune as they drifted off to their lockers and classes. Her opponent, Mark, was nowhere to be seen.

It took all day for each classroom to vote and for Mr. Arnold to tally the results. Julie caught herself staring at the loudspeaker on the wall, willing it to call them down to the assembly where Mr. Arnold would announce the winner. At last, the familiar crackle came over the PA system, and Julie heard the vice principal's voice.

"Students, we have the results of the election that you've all been waiting to hear. Starting with grade one, please make your way down to the gymnasium as quietly as possible."

As soon as they were seated, Julie asked Joy, "What's the sign for *butterflies*?"

Joy crossed her hands, linking her thumbs and wiggling her fingers.

Julie made the sign for *butterflies* and then pointed

to her stomach to show Joy how nervous and excited she felt.

Joy gave her a thumbs-up, wishing her good luck.

Mr. Arnold stepped up to the podium. "In all my years as head of student government, this has been one of the most exciting school elections at Jack London Elementary. All the candidates did an outstanding job and certainly gave us a lot to think about. There can only be one winner today, but everyone who participated in the election is a winner."

A first grader in the front row blurted out, "Teacher, who won? The boy or the girl?" The students burst out in laughter.

Mr. Arnold smiled. "To answer that question—" he paused for dramatic effect, and then went on—"I would like to extend my sincere congratulations to the 1976 Jack London Elementary student body president and vice president, Miss Julie Albright and Miss Joy Jenner! Please join me on the stage." The audience erupted with applause.

Julie and Joy hugged each other and then ran up the steps onto the stage to shake hands with Mr. Arnold. When the applause died down, the students in Class 5D suddenly rose to their feet, a small oasis in the center of the audience. Their hands, like fluttering leaves, waved in silent celebration as they applauded in sign language.

Looking out over the sea of teachers, classmates, and friends, Julie thought about all the changes the past year had held for her—a new school, a new home, and hardest of all, a new way of being a family. She smiled wistfully, remembering how hard it had been, at first, to stop wishing things would somehow go back to the way they used to be. But over the past year, she had learned that she didn't have to be afraid of change. It was different, and it was sometimes sad, even painful—but it was also an invitation to think new thoughts, to see things in a new way, to grow. Even to become a better person.

And all the changes had brought her to this moment—student body president.

Suddenly, T. J. dashed up onto the stage and yanked on a dangling rope. Bright balloons and confetti fluttered down, magically swirling around her.

"T. J., how on earth did you pull that off?" Julie asked him, laughing.

"Oh, Mr. Arnold and I had it all planned, no matter who won. But I had my fingers crossed that it would be you." He batted at a balloon and gave her a cocky grin. "This is how they do it for real when the president gets elected. One day that's going to be me—campaign manager for the president of the United States."

"You're hired!" said Julie. "When I run for president someday, there's nobody I'd rather have running my campaign."

INSIDE Julie's World

In Julie's time, Americans were starting to understand
that the environment needed protection from humans.
As people gained awareness of air and water pollution,
they began to see that simply setting natural areas aside
in parks and preserves was not enough to protect them.

The bald eagle was one of many species that needed
special protection. With their seven-foot wingspans,
bald eagles flew into power lines and were electrocuted.
They ate animals wounded by lead shot from hunters
and got lead poisoning. Their eggshells were weakened
by a pesticide called DDT. And they were running out of
places to nest. Bald eagles live in tall trees near oceans,
lakes, or rivers—valuable real estate where people like
to have homes. Around the time of Julie's story, a survey
found only 708 breeding pairs of bald eagles in the entire
mainland United States.

Through the protections of the Endangered Species
Act, which was enacted by Congress in the early seven-
ties, and the efforts of wildlife biologists and countless
volunteers like Julie and Robin, the bald eagle has made
a comeback and is one of the environmental movement's
biggest successes.

A few years after Americans created Earth Day, in
1970, they celebrated America's two-hundredth birthday.
On July 4, 1976, cities and towns across the country threw
Bicentennial picnics, parties, and parades.

Some people questioned whether the nation's founding was something to celebrate at all. Native American communities in particular were divided, and some chose to honor Indian history and culture instead. Others thought that the money spent on the Bicentennial would be better spent on serious problems like poverty. Still others wondered whether Americans, so deeply divided after the wounds of Watergate and Vietnam, could come together in celebration.

The summer of 1976 proved that they could—that Americans loved their country in spite of its problems and felt connected to their fellow citizens despite their differences. In the fall of that same year, many Americans saw the presidential election as an opportunity for change and felt Carter represented a change in leadership and a new direction for America.

The desire to make the world a better place—which Julie shows in her stories and many real Americans shared during the 1970s—is still alive today. While the country still faces serious problems, Americans of all ages, races, abilities, and political viewpoints continue to tackle these issues with optimism and creativity. They don't always agree with one another, but they usually share the same basic goal—to make their country truly a place of justice, freedom, and equality.

Read more of JULIE'S stories,
available from booksellers and at *americangirl.com*

❧ *Classics* ❧
Julie's classic series, now in two volumes:

Volume 1:
The Big Break
Julie's parents' divorce means a new home, a new school, and new friends. Will Julie ever feel at home in her new life?

Volume 2:
Soaring High
As Julie begins to see that change can bring new possibilities, she sets out to make some big changes of her own!

❧ *Journey in Time* ❧
Travel back in time and spend a day with Julie!

A Brighter Tomorrow
Step back into the 1970s and help Julie win her basketball game, save a stranded sea otter, and clean up the beach! Choose your own path through this multiple-ending story.

❧ *Mysteries* ❧
More thrilling adventures with Julie!

Lost in the City
Julie's taking care of a valuable parrot—and it's disappeared.

The Silver Guitar
A guitar from a famous rock star leads Julie and T. J. into danger.

The Puzzle of the Paper Daughter
A note written in Chinese leads Julie on a search for a long-lost doll.

The Tangled Web
Julie meets a new friend who isn't who she seems to be.

❀ *A Sneak Peek at* ❀

A Brighter Tomorrow

My Journey with Julie

Meet Julie and take an unforgettable journey in a book that lets *you* decide what happens.

H*onk honk, beep beep beep!* This city noise is so loud! I shut the window and curl onto the window seat. I had a window seat in my old room at our house in Ohio. We just moved to this apartment in San Francisco a week ago, and I'm still getting used to the view outside my window. Through the treetops I can see a whole row of colorful Victorian houses. Back in Ohio, houses are mostly white or beige; here in San Francisco, they are colorful, with fancy trim that looks like frosting on a cake.

I close my eyes for a moment and pretend I'm back in Ohio. If I concentrate hard enough, I can almost hear my dad singing oldies in the kitchen as he prepares my favorite breakfast: banana chocolate-chip pancakes.

"What're you doing?" My little brother's voice snaps me out of my daydream.

"Ever heard of knocking?" I ask him.

Zack shrugs. "Your door was open." He flops down on my bed and twirls a section of his curly brown hair just above his ear with his fingers. He does that whenever he's feeling anxious about something. Lately he does it a lot.

"Zack, you're going to get a bald spot. Pretty soon you'll be as bald as Dad!"

Zack swallows. "I miss Dad. I want to go home."

"Zack, we've been over this a gazillion times," I tell him. "This is home now. And Dad will be here before you know it." But I understand how Zack feels. I don't think this little apartment in the middle of California will ever feel like home.

Ever since Dad lost his job over six months ago, he and Mom have been arguing more than usual. When Mom got the job offer in California, my parents decided Dad would stay in Ohio to take some computer training courses so that he can find a good job when he moves to San Francisco. Mom told us it was a good time for them to "take a little vacation from each other."

Zack starts twirling his hair again. "I hate it here," he says, his face tightening. I can tell that he's trying not to cry. "Are Mom and Dad going to get a divorce?"

I pretend I didn't hear him and act as if I'm looking at something really interesting outside. I don't like to talk about these things, and I really don't like to even *think* about the *D* word: divorce.

Zack throws a pillow at me. "Did you hear me? I asked if Mom and Dad—"

"Look, Zack!" I say, pointing out the window.

"It's a bulldog! You love bulldogs!"

He wipes his cheek with the back of his hand and gazes at me with a hard look in his eyes. "Why won't you talk to me?" he asks. "Do you like it here?"

Of course not! I want to tell him. *I'm just as sad as you!* But I don't say it, because Zack's depending on me to be the big sister. And isn't a big sister supposed to stay strong and pretend that everything is fine? Besides, what does Zack know? He's just a little kid.

I give him a forced smile. "You know what? Let's go get some of those mini muffins that you love at that coffee shop downstairs. And a chocolate shake!"

Zack heaves a sigh. "Just forget it," he mumbles and shuffles out of my room.

A warm tear rolls down my cheek. I get up, thinking about going to tell him how I really feel, but I have no idea what I would say. *Maybe later,* I tell myself.

I slump heavily back onto the window seat. The cushion shifts under me and as I go to adjust it, I feel some hinges where the seat meets the wall. Does the seat open? I toss the cushion onto my bed and lift the lid to look inside. Among the dust and icky cobwebs, I find one dangly peace-sign earring, a nail clipper, a yellow butterfly barrette, and a half-dollar from 1975. It's as if I've found a time capsule!

I stand up to snap the barrette in my hair and put all of the other treasures in my pocket. I'm about to close the lid when something shiny catches my eye in the corner of the open window seat. A marble? A button? No, it's a ring, with a big black stone. I pick it up and slip it on, and as I admire the ring on my hand, the stone begins to lighten in color. Is it one of those mood rings?

Just then, the room starts to spin. I close my eyes, trying to make it stop. Then my stomach drops and it feels as if I'm falling. I land with a thud and open my eyes.

Oddly, I'm still sitting on the window seat—but everything has changed. The room looks like my room, but all my stuff has been replaced with someone else's. Beaded curtains and a scalloped canopy hang around the bed. A lava lamp sits on the desk, next to an old-fashioned record player and tape recorder. On the dresser is a framed picture of a family with two parents, a teenage girl, and a girl around my age. That girl has long blonde hair with a little braid down the side and sparkly dark-brown eyes. Could this be the blonde girl's room?

How did I get here? I was sitting on the window seat

in my new room one moment and then—*whoosh*—I ended up in this strange place. I glance down at the mood ring, which has turned a cloudy amber color. It seemed almost as if the . . . transformation, or whatever it was— happened when I put on the ring. This mood ring seems to do more than show moods; it shows other places!

I decide to explore this strange world beyond the bedroom. As I step onto the sidewalk, I notice a van parked nearby on which someone has painted *flower power* in colorful, swirly letters. A teenage boy with long shaggy hair and a tie-dyed shirt leans against the van. A woman with a puffy velvet cap, a leather vest, and a long skirt passes me on the street. She smiles at me and holds up her fingers in a peace sign.

Feeling disoriented, I look up at our apartment building. It's definitely the same building on the corner of Redbud and Frederick that Mom, Zack, and I just moved into. At least the street signs have the same names. I look to see if the coffee shop on the corner is there, but just as I suspected, it isn't. Instead there's a little boutique with a sign above the door that says Gladrags.

A little bell jingles as I step into the shop. It must be some kind of vintage thrift store. There are retro clothes on the racks, purses made out of blue jeans, and colorful beaded belts. A friendly woman about my mom's age gives me a warm smile as she helps a customer at the cash register. "Welcome to Gladrags," she says. "Feel free to have a look around."

"Thanks," I say. I pretend to study a display of seashell night-lights while I try to figure out what's going on. Just then, a girl with long blonde hair pops up from behind the counter and greets me with a big smile. It's the girl from the photo on the dresser.

"Hi," the blonde girl says.

The woman at the register clears her throat. "Julie, why don't you see if our customer needs help finding anything?"

"Oh, right!" the girl says. She scurries around the counter with a basketball under her arm. "I'm Julie. Julie Albright. This is my mom's shop. Are you looking for anything special?"

"Um, just browsing," I tell her. Really, I'm looking for a clue that might tell me where I am and what's going on. But I can't exactly say that, or she'd think, just like the kids at my new school, that I'm a weirdo.

About the Author

MEGAN MCDONALD grew up in a house full of books and sisters—four sisters, who inspire many of the stories she writes. She has loved to write since she was ten, when she got her first story published in her school newspaper. Megan vividly remembers growing up in the 1970s, from making apple-seed bracelets to learning the metric system. San Francisco is close to home for Megan, who lives with her husband in Sebastopol, California, where she writes the Judy Moody series and many other books for young people.